# Vampire of St Michan's

# Vampire of St Michan's

Don Conroy

Published 2001
by Poolbeg Press Ltd.
123 Grange Hill, Baldoyle
Dublin 13, Ireland
Email: poolbeg@poolbeg.com
www.poolbeg.com



1 3 5 7 9 10 8 6 4 2

A catalogue record for this book is available from the British Library.

ISBN 1 84223 085 9



Cover design by Steven Hope
Typeset by Patricia Hope in Goudy 11.5/16.5
Printed by Cox & Wyman

To David

# Author's Note

St Michan's Church, Church Street, is one of the oldest churches in Dublin and for a long time was the only church north of the Liffey. The church dates back to 1095. Some say it was built on the ruins of a Danish church and tradition has it that it was named after a Danish saint. Its fine square tower provides a landmark that can be seen from a great distance. The church has a magnificent organ which was built in 1724 by Baptist de Couville of Dublin. It is said that Frederick Handel practised on it prior to the first production of his Messiah in the city of Dublin. The organ was completely restored in 1952. Also to be seen is a magnificent wooden carving of seventeen musical instruments, carved from a single piece of wood. It was crafted in 1724 at a cost of £8. However, the most remarkable feature of the church is the vaults with its mummies. Though the church was originally built on marshy ground the air in the vault is very dry, the temperature remaining constant all year round. Apparently the dry air and the methane content in it act as a preservative. Visitors can tour the vaults and perhaps shake the hand of the oldest mummy there who is allegedly a knight. There is a graveyard in the grounds of the church. It is believed that the famous executed Irish leader, Robert Emmet, is secretly buried there. The funeral service of another remarkable Irishman, Charles Stewart Parnell, was held in St Michan's before he was interred in Glasnevin Cemetery.

If you visit this remarkable church I don't guarantee any vampires but I do guarantee that you will be reminded of Dublin's great and troubled past.

PS – The church is open only from March to October for tours/visitors.

# Chapter 1

Dublin, November 17th 1986

"How much do you have?" asked Sam Whelan.

"Well, it wasn't my idea to put eighty quid on a bet this afternoon," Pete growled.

"That horse was supposed to be a sure thing. I got the tip from Henno and he usually comes up trumps."

"I should have known," sighed Pete, "with a horse called 'Gone West'. I think it's still going west!"

Sam looked skywards. He could see a ring around the moon. He blew on his hands.

"It's freezing," he complained.

"We can't go into the Coach House," Pete grumbled. "We've a tab of at least seventy-five quid running there. If we show our faces O'Dwyer will be down our throats looking for the money."

Sam nodded glumly. "We've got to do something."

"I'm not breaking into no houses," said Pete, pointing a

finger at him. "Last time we did that we got six months in prison."

"How was I to know it would be a policeman's house? And a sergeant at that!"

They walked over O'Connell Bridge. Icy winds blew up along the Liffey.

"That wind would skin you," said Sam. He stopped his friend by placing his hand on his chest. "Listen, you've given me an idea."

"I told you –"

"Hear me out," Sam insisted. "I'm not asking you to break into anyone's house."

"Well, what? Tell me before I freeze to death."

"Let's go for a cup of tea and a plate of chips in Angelo's café. I'll explain there."

They were grateful to be out of the chilly winds. The café was warm and the smells were delicious to their nostrils. There were only a few customers on this cold night. They ordered and the waitress returned quickly with their food. They were given generous portions of chips and a big pot of tea with white bread on the side. They spread tomato ketchup thickly over their chips and plenty of salt and vinegar.

"Well, what's your great idea?" asked Pete.

"I was reading this article in a magazine about buried treasure and remarkable finds."

"That's great," said Pete. "You want us to go out and dig up some treasure chest, sure! Only where do we look? The Ring of Kerry perhaps!"

"Listen," said Sam, "people have found chalices in fields, gold coins under old buildings, rare gems in attics . . ."

"I'm sure there's a relevance to our situation in all this," sighed Pete.

"There is," said Sam enthusiastically. "What church do we pass on our way home every night?"

"You're not asking me to break into a church! I'll never stoop that low!"

"I'm not asking you to break into a church – exactly."

"What do you mean – exactly?"

"We pass by one of the oldest and most historic churches in Dublin every night."

"Which one is that?" asked Pete.

"St Michan's, of course. Below the church are vaults. They date back to the Vikings."

Pete laughed. "You don't want me to steal one of those mummies!"

"You're not listening. I'm convinced some of those bodies must have been buried with swords, jewellery, purses of gold. They did that kind of thing in the old days. So the person could have his or her favourite things with them in the next life."

"Surely someone would have found all that stuff by now," offered Pete.

"No," said Sam. "According to this article they found a Roman grave in York last year. They reckon it was a centurion from the Roman army. They found a sword, several bags of gold and a helmet worth a fortune." Pete finished the last of the chips and poured himself another cup of tea.

"Well, what do you think?" asked Sam impatiently.

"You're on," Pete grinned. "We've nothing to lose and everything to gain."

"Great! We'll have to go home and pick up a torch and a few tools. We'll need a hacksaw for the locks."

It was after eleven before they reached St Michan's. All was quiet around Church Street. The graveyard was covered with a light frost that clung to the grass and the ivy.

"Which way?" asked Pete after they had climbed over the railings into the church grounds.

"To the left," Sam beckoned.

"This place is very spooky at night," said Pete.

"Look, there's the entrance to the vault." Sam pointed at the iron door by the side wall.

The screeching of the hacksaw as it cut through the lock seemed very loud in the still night.

"Hurry," said Sam as he looked about for any signs of trouble.

"Finished," said Pete proudly, pulling the bolt across and lifting back the door. "Shine the torch down."

They could see the steps that led down to the floor of the vault.

"It's a bit creepy," Sam admitted as he descended the steps.

Pete reluctantly followed after him. He put on garden gloves and began to feel about in the first chamber.

"I found something," he whispered. It was an old coffin nail.

"Great," said Sam. "Just what I always wanted."

They continued to search each chamber down the long passageway, finding nothing but bits of old leather and velvet.

"Nothing," complained Pete. "Here, give me that torch. I think I see something."

Something glinted in the furthest chamber on the right side. They passed through an iron gate which luckily was open. "Bull's-eye! Now this is more like it." He held up a crucifix and rubbed it with his sleeve. "A solid silver cross!"

"I'm sure that's worth a few quid," said Sam. "Hey, here's another one. This one is even fancier. There must be some clergyman buried here."

"And another one," said Pete. "This one looks like it's brass."

Sam examined it. "You know, I think it might even be gold," he said excitedly.

"That coffin looks in good nick. The coffin handles are old brass and very ornate. We could sell them. No problem."

Pete took out a pliers and a screwdriver. "I'm going to check inside it. I'd say whoever was buried here had money."

"Let's hope he took it with him," Sam chuckled. They lifted back the lid without much difficulty. "Look," said Sam. He picked up a circular object that had fallen to the ground. "It's like a sacred host."

They shone the torch on the body inside the coffin. It was of a man. He looked like he was in his thirties and was dressed in fancy clothes.

"Wow, this body is in remarkably good condition," said Pete.

"It's something to do with the air down here," said Sam. "I remember reading about it once. Hey, look at the fancy rings on his fingers and the gold chain around his neck. Pete, we've struck it rich!"

Pete laughed. "We're like Burke and Hare, the grave-robbers of the nineteenth century. Except we're not stealing bodies, just jewellery he won't miss." They removed the necklace from around the neck. One ring came off without much trouble. The other proved more difficult to remove.

"Here, let me," said Pete. He got the pliers and, gripping the finger, he squeezed it in order to break it.

The eyes of the corpse opened and stared up at him.

Sam started and shone the torch on the face. Amber eyes stared back. They both screamed in terror. Pete slammed the coffin lid back down and as fast as their legs could move they ran down the passageway, then up the stairs to safety.

Pete kicked the iron door shut and bolted it. They stood there panting. "My God," he said, breathing hard, "did you see that?"

"Did I?" said Sam. "I nearly had a heart attack. Did you get the stuff?"

"It's all in the bag," grinned Pete. "Let's get the hell out of here."

They scrambled over the railings and ran down the road.

"I've heard of cases like that," said Sam as they hurried along the quiet streets, "people buried alive and coming around after. There's a name for it but I just can't remember it."

"Maybe we should report it," said Pete.

"Listen," said Sam, "we don't want to walk ourselves into a whole load of trouble. Besides the dress on that dead bloke was like what you'd see in one of those period pictures. I'm sure it must have been some sort of spontaneous reaction when we disturbed the corpse."

"Yeah, you're probably right," said Pete. "We'll leave him to rest" He grinned. "I can't wait to examine that stuff properly. We'll go to your place."

In the blackness of the vault the vampire stirred slowly. The coffin lid swung up and back. The figure inside rose up out of the ebony coffin, flexed his long sinewy figures and grimaced. "Free at last, free at last!" He laughed menacingly. His laughter echoed around the quiet chambers. "I've such a hunger, such a thirst," he spoke to the darkness. His eyes glowed like burning coals. "They who dared to steal from me shall be my first victims."

Pete and Sam sat at the small kitchen table in Sam's flat, which was on the top floor of a run-down Georgian house, drinking tea and cleaning up the objects they had stolen from St Michan's.

"These are lovely," said Pete, "and this chain is old gold. It must be worth a fortune. Feel the weight of it. It's very heavy." He slowly dropped it into Sam's cupped hand. Sam weighed it in his hand. "It's heavy all right. How much do you think it's worth?"

"I'd say at least a thousand smackers."

Sam smiled broadly, "A thousand pounds – now that's what I call a good night's work."

Outside in the darkness stood a tall figure in black. The vampire looked up at the light emanating from Sam's flat. He walked purposefully across the road to the Georgian house, looked around for any sign of movement, then like a giant spider began to climb effortlessly up the front of the building.

Sam put some briquettes on the fire while Pete made some more tea and toast for their supper. Then as Pete returned from the kitchen he saw a huge shadow passing outside the window. Then a figure appeared at the glass, its face pale, the eyes glowing red, a horrific grimace on the mouth. There was a terrible sound of breaking glass. With lightning speed the vampire had crashed through the window and, before Sam knew it, had grabbed him by the neck and with a violent jerk snapped his neck like a twig. Pete dropped the tray with their supper and grabbed a statuette from the mantelpiece to defend himself. The vampire knocked him to the ground, pinned his arms down and bit into his neck, drawing the lifeblood out of him. After a time he stopped, then moved over to feed on the lifeless form of Sam which lay, eyes open wide, on the floor.

The vampire stood up, feeling strong and satisfied. He picked up his neck chain and his ring. Wiping his mouth, he left by the door and walked down the many flights of stairs, undid the latch and walked out the front door into the cold night. He was once again, the most deadly of hunters, set free in a brand new century.

# Chapter 2

## Present Day

Doyler sat clutching a large styrofoam cup, half full of tea. He checked his watch, "Ten past four," he sighed. "They were supposed to be here at twelve thirty. Surely the plane has landed by now."

"What's that?" asked an old woman who was sitting nearby.

"Oh, just talking to myself," he replied.

"I do that myself sometimes," said the old woman. "I put it down to the fact that I live on my own. Do you?"

"Yes," said Doyler as he gulped down the rest of the tea.

She watched him place the empty cup alongside four other empty ones. "You've been waiting a while I see."

"Yes," said Doyler. "I got here bright and early. They were due at twelve thirty but still no sign of my passengers," he complained. "Of course, if I'd arrived late they'd be waiting for me. Murphy's Law."

"Where are your family coming from?" the woman enquired.

"Oh, they're not family," he grinned. "Not even friends, more like business associates. They're coming from Budapest."

"That sounds very grand altogether," said the old woman. "I'm waiting on my sister – she's coming from Manchester. Decided to come home at last –"

"Would you like a cup of tea?" asked Doyler. "I'm going to get one for myself."

"Oh, that would be very nice. Weak, with milk and two spoons of sugar."

"Right, be back in a jiffy."

He ordered two teas and two Danish pastries, then looked at the screens – still no mention of planes arriving from Budapest. He took out his mobile phone and phoned his friend Cooley Collins. "Cooley, it's me, Doyler. I'm stuck out at the airport. I've been waiting here all bloomin' day for Doctor Drachler and Madame Kinski. They were supposed to be here at twelve thirty. What? What are you laughing at?" He listened and groaned. "Oh God, you're right! I'm a prize idiot. I thought it was twelve thirty after midday, not after midnight! God, I could cut my throat. OK, thanks, see you soon."

Doyler and the old woman had finished drinking yet another cup of tea.

"Tea is much nicer made in a pot, don't you agree?"

Doyler nodded.

"I find airports can be very sad betimes."

"Boring betimes as well," he retorted.

At last the Manchester plane arrived. They watched the passengers being greeted by their friends and families, some laughing, some crying.

"You see the gamut of emotions from A to Z at airports," said Doyler.

"There she is," said the old woman brightly. She moved with surprising speed towards the arrivals gate. Doyler watched her hug another old woman who could've been her twin. They headed back towards him.

"This is my sister Abigail. This young man was very kind to me during my wait." Doyler beamed and shook her hand warmly.

"I haven't been called a young man for over twenty five years," he chuckled.

"Can't keep away from the ladies?" a voice boomed from behind.

Doyler turned to see his pal Cooley standing there, smiling broadly.

"Here, let us give you a hand with that luggage," said Cooley.

They helped the old ladies to an airport coach and watched them board.

"A right pair of canary birds," Doyler quipped as they waved them off.

"I think one of them fancied you," jeered Cooley.

"Give over," snapped Doyler.

"Let's get something to eat. I'm starving! I've been in Navan all morning delivering furniture."

Doyler scratched his stubble chin. "I could do with something substantial myself."

In the restaurant Doyler hurried over to one of the few empty tables. "Cooley, you get the food."

"Yes, Your Highness."

He brought back two plaice and chips, two sherry trifles and two pots of tea.

"Splendid," said Doyler. "I couldn't have made a better choice."

After the meal Doyler lit up a cigarette. Next thing a security man was telling him to put out the cigarette.

Doyle stubbed it out on his saucer. "They treat you like a leper these days if you smoke. I remember a time when you could smoke to your heart's content – nearly the whole country smoked then."

"Well, people nowadays are much more health-conscious," said Cooley. "Even my brother has stopped and he was like a chimney, always puffin'. Then one day he went to the doctor and the doctor told him –"

"Don't start about cancer or lung disease. It's too depressing."

"Right, but –"

"Let's stick to the business ahead. We haven't seen or

heard from Doctor Drachler for over two years. Then suddenly out of the blue he phones me."

"Didn't he send you a card from India last year?" Cooley reminded him.

"Oh yeah, he said he was writing some book about Hindu folklore or something like that."

"He's a bit odd but nice enough once you get to know him. Remember the last time he was here and all that business about the vampire?"

"Don't talk to me," said Doyler. "Every time I think about it, it puts the wind up me. To this day I don't know whether it was real or just some headbanger with a morbid fixation with bloodsuckers." He finished his tea. "Any more in your pot?"

Cooley poured him a drop. "That's the last of it."

"Would you not put the pot under your arm and squeeze it?" Doyler grinned. "Come on. Let's go down to the bar."

After a couple of pints of Guinness, Doyler sat back and closed his eyes. In a few moments he was fast asleep.

"Wake up!" Doyler could feel himself being shaken by the shoulder. He blinked open his eyes.

"Can a fellow not grab forty winks without being interrupted?" he complained.

"Forty winks," laughed Cooley. "You've been asleep nearly three hours."

Doyler rubbed his eyes and checked his watch. It was eleven thirty pm.

"Well, I must have needed it." He stretched and yawned.

"You were like a foghorn snoring away there – cleared out half the customers by your sounds." Cooley began to mimic his snoring.

"Give over," said Doyler.

After a time Cooley checked the screens. "It's landed," he said with relief.

"Let's go," said Doyler. "We don't want to be late after all this waiting around." People clustered at the arrival area. The level of noise rose as the waiting crowd watched the passengers pour into arrivals. An air of expectancy filled the area. Doyler and Cooley stared in eagar anticipation, for any contact with Doctor Drachler usually resulted in them making a lot of money.

Doyler's eyes were drawn to a woman who had come into the arrivals area. Her entrance commanded attention. "I wonder is that her?"

"She looks a bit of class," Cooley remarked.

The woman strode purposefully through the crowd. Her raven-black hair was pulled back and tied in a bun. She moved with grace, her fluid movements reminding one of a ballet dancer. She wore a long black coat with a hood that was surrounded by iron-grey wolf fur. Black leather boots showed where the coat swayed open at the legs.

There was no sign of the Doctor. The woman suddenly stopped and scanned the waiting area, then her eyes rested on them. She beckoned them over.

"Doyle and Collins, is it not?"

"Yes, Ma'am, Madame," blurted Doyler.

"Frederika Kinski." She extended her black-gloved hand in greeting, all the while holding them in her gaze.

Doyler didn't know whether to shake her hand or kiss it. Taking it, he shook it warmly.

"My luggage is over there," she said, pointing towards the arrivals entrance.

"Cooley, get the lady's luggage!" said Doyler, snapping his fingers.

He stared at Madame Kinski, fascinated. Her face was unnaturally pale, the red lipstick exaggerating this. Her eyes were utterly penetrating. She wore a golden brooch on her coat, shaped like a dagger, ancient in appearance, with some symbols on the blade. Her voice and attitude commanded immediate respect.

"I am so pleased to be in your beautiful country. I love old cultures – their roots are very deep."

"Oh yes," said Doyler, "we're an old race, been around a long time. We have a place called Newgrange. Older than the pyramids."

"Wonderful. I must visit sometime," she remarked.

They headed for the exit, Cooley pushing the luggage-trolley.

"If you like to wait here," said Cooley, "I'll bring the van around. Save you walking."

"A van!" she exclaimed. "You can't be serious! You expect me to travel in a commercial vehicle?"

Doyler gave a quick glance at Cooley who looked skywards. He snorted and grinned "We were just kidding. You'll have to get used to the Irish humour."

"Kidding?" she asked.

"Fooling around, joking," he retorted. "The van is for your luggage," he added, thinking quickly. "We'll get a taxi outside."

"I only travel in limousines," she said sharply.

"Oh, there aren't too many limos in Ireland, a small country and all that," he smiled, hiding his stress.

"There, over there!" Cooley pointed at a Mercedes taxi.

She looked at the black Merc. "That will do fine."

Doyler gave a sigh of relief. "Follow me, Madame," he said, winking at Cooley.

"I was expecting Doctor Drachler to be with you," said Doyler as they drove to the hotel.

"He had business in London. He will be arriving in Dublin around midday tomorrow."

After a long silence Doyler piped up again. "You'll enjoy staying in the Shelbourne Hotel. A lot of famous people have stayed there over the years."

She put a cigarette into a cigarette holder. "Light me," she commanded.

Although there was a no-smoking sign in the cab, the driver didn't seem to mind. Doyler fumbled in his pockets and found a box of matches. He struck the match several times against the box before it lit up. "Must be a little damp." He grinned awkwardly. He too took out a cigarette and began to smoke.

A plume of blue smoke came from her red lips. "Do you like the night, Mr Doyle?" He was taken back by the question.

"Oh yeah, the day wouldn't be complete without it!" He grinned broadly.

She smiled at him. "Mr Doyle, you are something of a wit."

"I like to think so," he said, feeling rather pleased with himself.

She looked beyond him and spoke quietly. "There is a secret abyss that lies at the edge of darkness. A world beyond most human understanding. Some call it the hour of the wolf. The time when children are born and the old must die, where the dream invaders come to call and the other worlds open their secret gates. When night creatures walk in freedom . . ." She stopped. She put out her cigarette and looked at him. "Thank you, Mr Doyle, for collecting me. Call me when we arrive at the hotel. I'm going to rest now."

Doyler watched her as her eyelids slid down slowly. He

couldn't help but admire her. A woman of remarkable pale beauty. She rested in statuette stillness.

The journey was relatively quick compared to struggling through the choking Dublin traffic in daylight hours. As they pulled up in front of the hotel and the engine was switched off, Doyler nervously reached over to awaken her. But before his hand reached her shoulder, she opened her brown eyes – they were bright and alert in an instant.

"We've arrived at your hotel," Doyler said.

She stepped out briskly and moved towards the hotel entrance.

Cooley arrived in the Hi-ace van and parked behind the Mercedes. Doyler waved at Cooley to come out. "I'd better go and check she gets settled in okay – you know how fussy these foreigners can be. Pay the taxi man like a good lad and I'll be back down in a minute."

"Why me?" Cooley complained.

"You'll get it back," Doyler assured him.

"When? The next blue moon?" Cooley growled.

Doyler patted him on the shoulder. "That Madame in there is our meal ticket for the next month or more. Besides," he winked and elbowed him, "I'll get the fish and chips later."

"Great," Cooley sighed.

# Chapter 3

Dublin, 2001

The midnight hour approached. The streets were quiet. A taxi moved slowly along the wet roads. A heavy rainfall earlier had left puddles along the old pavements and the water had gathered over the blocked drains. Under the shadow of St Michan's Church a figure appeared from the side of the building near the entrance to the crypt. The figure moved in and out through the shadows. He moved silently down the street stopping briefly to check for sounds. A feral cat padded across the road carrying a dead pigeon in its jaws. The hum of traffic from O'Connell Street could be heard, though the quays were quiet as they had been blocked off for roadworks earlier that evening.

The night predator caught his first glimpse of his potential quarry, as they staggered up from the quays. He moved back into the shadows. He watched as the two men neared St Michan's, supporting each other.

"Manchester United is the finest team ever to have come out of England," one of the men declared as he stood rummaging in his pockets.

"Come on, Jimmy," said the other. "I need to get my head down. I've an early start in the morning."

Jimmy placed both his hands on his friend's shoulders. "Listen, Bobby, in life you must take time to smell the roses . . . if you take my meaning. Tomorrow is another day. Now as I was saying . . ." he slurred his words. "What was I saying, Bobby?"

"You were saying how great United are."

Jimmy prodded his finger into Bobby's chest "Exactly. Great is the word."

"What about Spurs?" asked Bobby, who was just as drunk as his friend.

"I'm not saying they didn't have their moments of glory," Jimmy retorted, "but their days of glory are over, gone. Just a memory, you know what I mean?" He was trying to light up a cigarette.

Bobby began to gesture broadly with his arms. "How can you stand there and say Spurs are rubbish?"

"Hold on now, Bobby, and don't be puttin' words in my mouth. I simply said –"

The vampire, from the darkened door, moved with lightning speed towards the men, rushing on one while knocking the other clean off his feet. At the powerful blow Bobby fell into the wet gutter, not knowing what had hit him. As he staggered to his feet he recoiled in horror. Jimmy, his friend, stood struggling and kicking as some fiend gripped him from behind and seemed to be biting him on the neck. Bobby got up and rushed at the attacker who simply dodged and delivered another vicious blow to the back of his neck that sent him crashing face down on the road, stunned. Then the stranger grimaced, opened his mouth wide and chomped down again on Jimmy's neck. His helpless victim shrieked loudly as he buried his fangs deeper. After a few minutes he withdrew his mouth. Jimmy's body lay limp, eyes rolled back in their sockets. The vampire threw the body to the ground and turned his attention to Bobby who was trying to stand up. He pulled his head back by the hair and buried his fangs into his neck, satisfying his bloodlust once more.

Then, checking that the coast was clear, he lifted the body up and hid it below an iron stairway. Picking up the other body from the road, he flung it over his shoulders as if it were a mere scarf. Headlights pierced the darkness. The vampire ducked into an archway. The car turned up a side street. When things became quiet again the vampire carried Jimmy's body down to the quays and threw it into the River Liffey. There was a loud splash but no one was around to hear on this cold wet night. The body floated for a time and then sank below the surface. The vampire grinned, feeling he was getting stronger as the warm blood coursed through his veins. They were soft targets. He would have preferred younger men or women without the stench of alcohol and tobacco on them. He went back, got the other body and dumped it in the river alongside the first.

This had been his first attack since he'd arrived back in Dublin after an absence of several years. Since those foolish thieves had broken into the crypt and accidentally set him free, he had been yearning to visit his old haunts – Paris, Rome, Brussels and Berlin. They all had changed dramatically since he'd stalked the streets in the late nineteenth century. Horses had been replaced by cars. Some of the elegant buildings had been torn down and replaced by giant glass boxes. Fashions too had changed and not for the better in his opinion. One thing that hadn't changed was humans but there were many more of them which was all the better for a bloodsucker like himself; and they all had warm crimson nectar running through their veins . . .

Now that his hunger was sated he walked the streets, familiarising himself with the layout of the city. This he did wherever he travelled. There was an atmosphere he liked in Dublin, an old-world feeling that lay behind the modern facades. The city's roots were deep and old like himself. In his travels he had met a few of his kind, usually in the larger cities. There they could have a certain anonymity. Since most humans didn't believe in his kind, the modern world made things a lot easier for vampires. The ones who did acknowledge their existence were few and they had a lot of misconceptions about his kind. That vampires could not walk about in daylight and were afraid of running water and the like. It amused him to ponder on these ideas. The humans must have got the notions from books or other such materials.

# Chapter 4

The following day Doyler headed once again to the airport, this time to collect Doctor Drachler who was due in from London. The traffic was chronic. It took him over half an hour to clock up three miles. He snorted in frustration. When he finally reached the airport the plane had landed.

He hurried to the arrivals area and within minutes Doctor Drachler was briskly exiting through the doors. The Doctor was very distinguished: tall, slim, with silvery grey hair swept back and now sporting a well-shaped beard. He was very tanned, making his eyes seem even more piercing than usual.

"Doctor Drachler! Over here!" Doyler waved.

The Doctor came towards him, extending his hand. "Doyle! Good to see you again." They shook hands. The Doctor had a warm expression on his face. Doyler had remembered a more severe countenance.

Drachler tapped Doyler in the stomach. "I see you're not fading away," he smiled.

"No, sir, I need the extra reserves for all the work I do," Doyler retorted, picking up the Doctor's leather travel case.

Drachler held on to his hand luggage.

"Hope you don't mind travelling by van, Doctor?"

"Well, it will be a first for me," he smiled.

When the Doctor sat into the van his head was almost touching the roof of the vehicle.

"Sorry about this, my friend. Cooley has the car."

"Oh, how is he?" the Doctor enquired.

"Never better," said Doyler. "You'll be seeing him later." He looked down at the remains of a ham sandwich on the floor near the Doctor's shining leather shoes. He hoped to God that the Doctor didn't step on it. He gritted his teeth. Why hadn't he got a taxi. The thought raced through his head. It would have been quicker and cleaner – and the Doctor would be paying for it eventually. 'You're a skinflint,' he scolded himself.

"Terrible all the business about the foot-and-mouth disease in Britain," the Doctor remarked, glancing at the headlines of The Times.

"Ah shocking," said Doyler. "Still, it hasn't put me off my rashers and sausages!" He guffawed loudly.

"Indeed!" The Doctor returned to reading, then after a moment enquired, "I trust you collected Madame Kinski and that she is settled into the hotel?"

"Oh indeed," said Doyler. "A beautiful woman if I may say so. Very regal-like too. Well, what do you say, Doctor? I think we should take a little trip to Bewley's. Remember the place we first met? Of course the museum is closed. They've jazzed the place up a bit. I preferred it the old way, but the all-day breakfasts are still tops." His mouth watered at the thought.

They arrived at Bewley's on Grafton Street. Doyler bought a paper on the way in and ordered a hearty breakfast for himself and a coffee for Doctor Drachler. The Doctor seemed a changed man – more chatty and relaxed, Doyler thought. The two men sat back reading the papers: the Doctor The Times and Doyler the early edition of the Evening Herald.

Suddenly the Doctor sat up as he looked across at Doyler's paper. The headline read 'Bodies drained of blood.'

"What?" asked Doyler.

"Your paper, may I see it?"

"Sure," said Doyler.

The Doctor read: "Two middle-aged men were found drowned in the River Liffey in the early hours of this morning. Despite the fact that they were made redundant recently by the closure of the Aerbrite Plant, family and friends strongly deny any suggestions of a suicide pact. The bodies were discovered by a milkman doing his deliveries to local shops in the area. The police were baffled by the fact that the bodies appeared to be drained of blood." The Doctor heaved a deep sigh.

"Everything all right?" asked Doyler.

"Yes, fine, thank you. We should go and see how Madame Kinski is."

"You don't mind if I finish my breakfast first?" Doyler grinned.

They strolled to the Shelbourne Hotel and there they met Madame Kinski who was sipping coffee in the lounge.

"My dear Alex, lovely to see you!" she exclaimed.

"And you." He kissed her on both cheeks.

"I trust you had a pleasant trip?"

"Oh, fine. No delays," he smiled.

"And how is Mr Doyle today?" she enquired.

"Never better, thanks."

"Let us take some air in that lovely park I spied from my bedroom."

"That's St Stephen's Green, Ma'am," said Doyler. He broke into song. " Dublin can be heaven with coffee at eleven and a stroll through Stephen's Green!"

She smiled broadly. "Charming, Mr Doyle." She opened her bag and put on a pair of dark sunglasses.

They walked around the park.

"Oh look, a robin!" She pointed at a branch eye-height where a male robin sang a few clear notes. "What's that one there?" she wondered as she watched a small bird move almost mouse-like at the base of the tree.

"It's a sparrow," said Doyler proudly.

"Well, to be precise," said Doctor Drachler, "it's a dunnock – also known as a hedge sparrow."

"Dublin is everything I had hoped for," she smiled, looking across at the Georgian buildings. "Now tell me, Alex, did you have any luck finding a suitable rented house for me?"

"I checked a number of websites and I'm sure the place I've arranged for you in County Wicklow will suit your requirements. It's a lovely old eighteenth-century farmhouse on twenty-five acres, tastefully restored a number of years ago. The owner is some wealthy movie star who lives in Hollywood – he visits only rarely."

"Oh, it sounds delightful! When do we see it?"

"Would this afternoon suit?"

"Splendid! You are a darling man." She kissed him on the cheek.

Doyler smiled. She must be the reason for the change in the Doctor's temperament, Perhaps he's in love with her, he mused. Then his mobile phone rang.

"Oops, sorry about this," said Doyler. "Hello? Brendan Doyle speaking."

"I know it's you," Cooley jeered from another mobile.

"Oh, good morning, Mr Collins," said Doyler in mock formality.

"Cut the bull," said Cooley. "Did you collect the old geezer?"

"Yes, Mr Collins, I collected the good Doctor this morning and we had a splendid breakfast in Bewley's – well, I did – he just had a coffee."

"Is that Cooley?" the Doctor enquired.

"Yes. Please hold the line for Doctor Drachler."

The Doctor took the mobile phone. "Hello, young Cooley, how are you? Well, I'm very pleased to hear it. I would like you to hire a car for me and bring it around to the Shelbourne at lunchtime and of course join us for lunch. Make sure it is a large comfortable car. I experienced a very different form of transport today." He laughed, "Yes, I came from the airport by van. It was a first for me and my back is not the better for the experience."

Doyler looked very embarrassed.

Frederika rubbed her gloved hand up and down the Doctor's back. "My poor darling, you should let me massage it for you."

"I'm fine," he smiled, handing the phone back to Doyler. "Right, you know what to do."

"Any particular colour?" asked Doyler of Madame Kinski.

"Now you are teasing!" laughed Frederika.

"What? Oh right. Excuse me, Doctor, Cooley was wondering if he could trouble you for your credit-card number? His own has recently expired."

The Doctor plucked out a gold card from his leather wallet and read out the number.

Doyler repeated it slowly. "Got that?" Then he stepped a few feet away from the others. "Glad you're paying for this call," he sniggered down the phone. "See you later."

"Oh, there's so much to take in, in a new city!" Frederika took a deep breath. She linked the two men as they walked around the park. Doyler felt very chuffed with himself, being so close to such a stunning and stylish lady. He could see how much more relaxed she was and he knew it must be because of the Doctor's presence.

Cooley arrived in a suitably large and comfortable car and joined them for lunch. Doyler and he felt rather awkward sitting down to lunch in such a fancy restaurant. Not that they didn't enjoy it, but it was difficult trying to work out all the cutlery on the white cotton tablecloth.

The Doctor sensed their hesitancy when the food arrived. "Work from the outside in," he said, picking up his cutlery.

Frederika took some tomato and basil soup and a glass of red wine into which she sprinkled a casket of powder, stirring it with a teaspoon. She did not eat any main course but seemed to enjoy a dark chocolate cake for dessert.

"That was a grand meal," said Doyler. "Not too much but very tasty."

Frederika smiled.

"If it isn't too forward, Miss," Cooley piped up, "what

line of work are you in? Or are you one of the idle rich?" he grinned. Doyler kicked him under the table. "I was just wondering . . ." He looked at Doyler.

"Thank you for enquiring." She paused, sipping her red wine. "I'm a writer of fiction, unlike my good friend the Doctor here," she placed her hand in his, "who writes wonderful books on so many interesting topics – from folklore and mythology to anthropology and archaeology."

"Dear Madame Kinski," the Doctor interjected, "writes bestsellers. She has received numerous awards, and has many admirers worldwide. Some of her books have been made into movies and television plays."

"Oh Alex! You sound like my agent!"

"I am," he laughed.

"What kind of books?" asked Doyler. "Maybe I've read some." He raised his cup of tea to his mouth and gulped it down.

She flashed a warm smile, showing her perfect pearly white teeth. "Vampire books."

The tea shot out of Doyler's mouth, staining the white tablecloth. He coughed loudly and Cooley patted him on the back.

"Are you all right, Mr Doyle? I didn't expect my response to have such an effect on you."

"No," he grinned, trying to recover, "something went against my breath but I'm fine now."

The waiter hurried over and began to clear up while

another arrived with a fresh white tablecloth. After the table was cleared and reset Doctor Drachler spoke quietly to Doyler.

"Madame Kinski is fully aware of our encounter with the vampire in Tintern Abbey, Co Wexford."

"Yes, I am." She smiled warmly. "In fact, the incident was so fascinating to me it became the basis for one of my novels, thanks to dear Alex." She leaned against him.

"Which book was that?" enquired Cooley.

"The Vampire of Ireland."

"Well, I'm glad something good came of that weird and terrifying experience!" said Doyler.

In the early afternoon they headed for County Wicklow. Beyond the valley of Roundwood village they took a winding road that cut through the hills. Taking a left and heading down a steep dirt track they could see a small wooded area. The woods opened out to a tree-lined avenue. As they drove up the road they could see an impressive eighteenth-century manor. They stopped the car in front of Morrigan Manor. Frederika stepped out and stretched her arms. "How delightful!"

Drachler smiled. "The manor comes with a manservant and two maids. They will be here at five o'clock. In the meantime we can make ourselves at home." He walked over towards a carved granite statuette of a griffin and reached behind it, then smilingly produced a large key.

Madame Kinski approached him and extended her hand, "May I?"

He handed her the key. She turned and looked back and smiled at Doyler and Cooley who now moved over to the Doctor. She ascended the seven steps, then hesitated a moment at the great studded oak door.

"She does have a most exquisite face, don't you agree?" Doctor Drachler remarked.

"Ah, she's a fine thing, no doubt about it," said Cooley.

"A what?" wondered Doctor Drachler.

Doyler nudged Cooley firmly. "What he means is that she's very attractive."

"Yes, very true," smiled the Doctor.

Frederika inserted the iron key, turned it in the lock, then pushed the door open. She stepped inside, the others hurrying up the stairs after her. She stood in the hallway, took a deep breath as if to drink in the experience, then moved briskly inside. She turned and beckoned to them, curling her fingers gracefully. They hastened forward.

She smiled. "I feel this house is infused with a warm presence." She gazed around the room. "I'm going to enjoy my stay here."

Cooley and Doyler took a sideways glance at each other.

"Shall I make some coffee?" asked the Doctor, heading to find the kitchen.

"Could I have tea, please?" said Doyler. "Since you're playing mother."

"Gentlemen, please sit down." Frederika sat in a leather armchair while Doyler and Cooley sat back into a sofa.

"Madame Kinski?" Doyler cleared his throat, a habit he had when he was nervous. She looked at him, her eyes utterly penetrating.

"Well," he stammered awkwardly, "I – we were wondering how exactly can we be of service to you during your stay?"

"All in good time, dear Doyler and Cooley, the Doctor will explain all in due course."

The Doctor soon arrived back with a tray laden with coffee, tea, cake and a single glass of water.

"A well-stocked kitchen," he declared as he lay the tray down and began to pour the coffee and then the tea.

He handed Frederika a glass of water. She smiled with her eyes, then took a sachet from her bag and sprinkled the contents into the water and stirred it with a spoon. The water changed to a dark crimson colour. Doyler and Cooley watched her drink it down in one gulp.

"A sort of medicine," she offered.

"I'll stick to the tea," Doyler grinned and helped himself to a slice of Madeira cake.

# Chapter 5

The young woman walked briskly down the dimly lit street. She had walked the streets hundreds of times from work to home but tonight she felt a strange sense of unease as if she was being followed. She turned and looked around, half-expecting to see someone behind her. Nervously, she pulled out her mobile phone and rang her boyfriend. She got his answering machine. She didn't leave a message. She would phone him when she got back to her apartment.

Her attention was suddenly drawn to what looked like a man standing on top of a roof up ahead. She stopped in disbelief. There was no mistaking it. He stood at the very edge of the roof of the Georgian house. 'What's he up to?' she wondered. It looked very precarious, in fact downright dangerous. A car passed by and she glanced away. When she looked back, she could see no sign of the man. Perhaps he was someone working late, putting up a satellite dish or repairing a roof. Ten o'clock seemed rather late to be working on a dark roof. She passed the row of terraced houses and gave another glance upwards at the roof. No sign of anyone.

Then her attention was drawn to what looked like a large black creature climbing down the side of the building – head first. Were her eyes playing tricks? She shrieked when she realised it was a man climbing down the side of the house, like a large black spider.

She ran down the road screaming and didn't stop until she reached her apartment. In her panic to find her door-key she spilled the contents of her bag onto the steps. Her phone fell to the basement below. She bent down and scrambled for her keys, then finding them she rammed the door-key into the lock.

Suddenly she felt a sharp pain to her head as a hand gripped her long fair hair. Another covered her mouth before she could scream. She tried to bite the hand. She felt herself being pulled helplessly backwards.

An old woman in a flat across the road was drawing her curtains when she saw what looked like a man pulling a woman down the laneway. She heard a scream. She hurried to her phone and rang the police. Outside the girl kicked and screamed but to no avail. A vicelike grip around her throat squeezed the life out of her. She slumped to the ground. The vampire grimaced, opened his mouth and clamped it on the soft skin, fangs piercing the flesh. He mantled her body like a bird of prey over its kill.

Minutes later a police siren could be heard piercing the night air. The squad car pulled to a halt. The old woman was already on the street pointing to the laneway. One policeman stayed with her while the other two hurried up the laneway. They found the young girl's body spread-eagled, two puncture marks on her throat.

Inspector Mark Wilson spread out the photos of the recent victim on his desk. He knew it was the same killer or killers as the body was drained of blood and had puncture wounds in the neck. Detective McGuire arrived into the office with a file of unsolved crimes from the eighties. "All this stuff is on the computer, you know, at the touch of a button."

"Pour us out some coffee and stop whingeing," the Inspector retorted.

Detective McGuire poured two coffees.

"I wonder is this some weird cult?" McGuire suggested.

"My thoughts exactly," said Wilson. He pored over the files from the eighties. "Eleven victims then, all drained of blood. Then the killing stopped in '87."

"Now 2001 and it's happening all over again. Sounds like the same psycho," McGuire remarked.

"What's with the blood loss?" Wilson wondered.

"Perhaps he or they are collecting blood to sell to some rich freak."

McGuire sipped his coffee. "Or perhaps it's a vampire," he grinned.

Wilson got up and closed the door to his office. "We don't want anyone listening to this conversation – they'll have us both certified."

"What I mean," said McGuire, "is that I reckon there's some nutter out there who is convinced he's a vampire, committed these crimes in the eighties, left the country and has now returned."

"I have a hunch you might be right," sighed Wilson. "Only don't even hint of this to anyone. Can you imagine what the papers would say if they got wind of it, I can just see the headlines 'Vampire Stalks Streets of Dublin'." He did up the knot in his tie and picked up his cellular phone. "Let's go for lunch." McGuire picked up the daily paper from the desk and followed after him.

Reporters waited at the front desk. "Anything for us, Inspector Wilson?"

He brushed past them, "Nothing lads, waiting for the forensic reports. We will keep you posted."

"You heard the Inspector," said the desk sergeant. "So, fellas, would you clear off so I can get back to my business at hand?"

The reporters rushed out after the two men. "Inspector, give us something for the morning edition!"

"Sorry, boys," said McGuire, "you'll just have to do the usual."

"What's that?" asked a reporter?

McGuire got into the squad car. "Make it up," he grinned. They drove away.

When they reached Molloy's pub they both relaxed in the lounge and ordered the braised beef special. McGuire scanned the back of the paper. His eyes were drawn to a heavy black-bordered advertisement. "Listen to this, Inspector! Here's a talk that might be just up our alley!"

"What are you rabbiting on about ?" said Wilson.

McGuire read aloud.

Irish Gothic Society
proudly presents
'The World of the Undead'
Vampires in myth, folklore and literature
with internationally acclaimed horror writer
Frederika Kinski and Doctor A Drachler,
eminent folklorist and historian
April 23rd, 7.30, Gresham Hotel
Admission £5
(includes light refreshments)

"Are you trying to wind me up?" asked Wilson.

The waitress arrived just then with two hot meals and they tucked into the food.

"Are you suggesting these vampire experts might have something to do with the murder?" asked Wilson.

"Well, no, Inspector," answered McGuire. "Probably not. But you must admit it's a strange coincidence. And they might be able to provide us with some useful information about vampire-lovers."

"Like a psychological profile?" The Inspector thought for a minute. Then he chuckled. "Right, get us some tickets and we can brush up on vampires!"

# Chapter 6

Doyler drove to the Gresham Hotel. Madame Kinski and Doctor Drachler sat in the back looking over their notes for the evening's lecture.

"How are you feeling?" Drachler enquired tenderly.

She looked up at him. "I'm fine," she said and kissed him.

Doyler spied them in the mirror and smiled to himself. He then watched as she took out what looked like a large silver disk. With a twist of her hand it opened out into a small silver goblet. Drachler took out a hip flask and poured what appeared to be red wine into it, then he held it while she sprinkled the contents of one of her sachets into it. Doyler was so busy watching what was going on that he nearly ran into a parked car up ahead. He swerved, narrowly avoiding another car, only to be confronted by a policeman who had seen the incident. The policeman raised his hand

and Doyler jammed on his brakes, making the car screech to a halt. Frederika just barely managed to prevent the contents of the goblet from spilling over her.

"What's the matter with you?" Drachler snapped at Doyler.

The policeman was ordering Doyler to roll down the window. Doyler did so and smiled awkwardly.

"Your driver's licence," said the policeman.

Doyler felt in his jacket pocket. He didn't have his driving licence but went through the motions anyway.

"Officer," said Doctor Drachler, "we are in rather a hurry. We have to give a lecture in the Gresham Hotel at half past seven."

"That's no excuse for reckless driving," the policeman said curtly.

Then Frederika leaned over. "Officer," she said softly, "I'm afraid I'm to blame. I distracted our driver."

The policeman bent over, their eyes met and he became locked in her gaze. Her eyes were utterly penetrating and her voice gentle and soothing. It was as if she had cast a spell over him; he was completely lost to her. He stepped back from the car as if in a hypnotic state. He waved them on.

Doyler gave a sigh of relief and drove on.

The Doctor kissed Frederika's hand. She smiled and laughed, then sat back and drank from the goblet, finishing the contents in one gulp.

"There's the hotel," said Doyler. "Up ahead on the right side of O'Connell Street."

Cooley was there to greet them as they entered the hotel lobby, a distinguished-looking man beside him.

"Madame Kinski, it is a great honour to meet you in person," said the man, extending his hand. "I am Michael Hamilton, Secretary to the Gothic Society."

She smiled and took his hand. "In my country we kiss on each cheek."

Hamilton smiled, a little embarrassed, then kissed her on each cheek.

"That wasn't too difficult," she smiled.

"Oh no, it was lovely. I mean delightful," he blurted. "Doctor Drachler, you're very welcome." He shook his hand, then Doyler's. He hurried them to a quiet part of the lobby where they sat down in comfortable armchairs. "We are all so looking forward to hearing your talk. There have been phone calls all day! I'd say we'll have a full house. Tea, coffee or something stronger?"

"Coffee is fine, thank you," said Frederika.

"And tea," Doyler added.

The Secretary welcomed the audience to their seventh annual public lecture, spoke briefly about the guest speakers, then listed the various books Madame Kinski had written, the awards she had received and the films that were made, based on her books. The enthusiastic crowd applauded loudly. The secretary was delighted to see it was almost a full house, certainly the most successful to date organised by the Society. He then went on to talk about the achievements of Doctor Drachler.

Doyler and Cooley sat to the side of the ballroom where the lecture was taking place. "People must have little to do with their time and money when they come to listen to some foreign bird talk about vampires," Doyler whispered to Cooley.

"It takes all kinds," said Cooley, "to make up the world. They probably think it's ridiculous people flocking to a football match to watch teams of men kick a leather ball of air around."

Detective McGuire, who was sitting in the fourth row from the front, spotted Inspector Wilson arriving. He waved to get his attention.

Wilson excused himself as he passed through the row of seated people. He took off his coat. "Could you not get any closer?" he quipped.

"Ah now, Chief, I wanted you to hear everything," McGuire smirked.

At that point the lights were dimmed in the ballroom and the stage lit brighter. Doctor Drachler was the first to speak. He stood at the lectern and put on his bifocal glasses. After thanking the Society and the audience for the warm welcome he began. “Down through the ages, people all over the world have made sacrificial offerings of blood to their various gods. The reason? To appease those moody gods and to keep evil spirits at bay. In Homer’s Odyssey the spirits of the dead spoke to Odysseus after drinking the sacrificial blood. In the Old Testament, Leviticus 17:14, it says ‘the life of the flesh is the blood’. Also in an earlier Hebrew text it states that the first woman created by God as a wife for Adam was Lilith. She soon got bored with Adam and went off to become queen of the demons and evil spirits and became a bloodsucker. In ancient times people placed an amulet in their babies’ cradles to protect them from the demon Lilith. The legend of Lilith has its source in ancient Babylonian myths. Eve, of course, became the second wife and we know what happened there,” he smiled. “The Greek and Roman myths have their fair share of bloodthirsty goddesses, Striges being the most common. These female demons would attack young babies or men while they slept. Whether those ancient myths and legends are the sources of the myths of the ‘undead’ or ‘vampire’ is open to debate. Some have traced the notion of the ‘nosferatu’, the ‘undead’, to ancient China, India, Malaysia, Polynesia as well as to the Aztecs and the Eskimos or Inuit. The European vampire had its genesis in ancient Greece . . .”

“This is all very interesting,” whispered Inspector Wilson to his colleague, “but it’s not bringing us any nearer to solving our cases.”

"Patience," McGuire retorted.

"In 1031, in a city in central France, the bishops of Cathor excommunicated a knight. The knight in question, according to one source, was already dead. But rumours started to spread throughout Cathor that the knight had been seen on several occasions wandering the night in search of human blood. England began to experience the curse of vampirism. Walter Map, the ecclesiastical scholar and wit, and William of Newburgh, an Augustinian monk, wrote works containing all manner of diabolic goings-on. Where caskets were found open and empty and then in the morning the bodies had returned to their place of rest, blood smeared across their mouths . . ."

Doyler cringed. "Do we have to stay here listening to all this?"

"They are paying us," said Cooley.

"Let's slip out for a while and head to Burdock's for the best fish and chips in Dublin."

Cooley looked at his watch.

"I'd say this will go on for at least an hour and a half more," Doyler assured him.

As Doyler and Cooley slipped quietly away they passed a tall man entering the hotel. Cooley held the door open for him. The man walked by, ignoring them. He had strikingly handsome features with black curling hair, and wore a long black coat with a red scarf hanging loosely around his neck.

"You're welcome," said Cooley sarcastically.

"Come on," said Doyler, "my stomach's growling."

The stranger sat in the lobby and ordered a glass of red wine. He drummed his fingers on the armrest and looked about as he drank it. He watched a young cleaner who was heading towards the toilets. Nearby an elderly couple were dozing in the plush armchairs. The newspaper was opened across the man like a blanket. The stranger stood up, finished the glass of wine, left a five-pound note and crossed to the toilets. Inside the young Spanish cleaner was spraying the mirror with glass cleaner. He did not hear the stranger enter. He began to wipe the glass, removing fingermarks and soap splashes. Soon it was gleaming. He looked at himself in the mirror and checked his teeth for a particle of food trapped between them which was causing him discomfort. As he did so, he suddenly became anxious and the hairs on the back of his neck began to bristle. There was no apparent reason for this. There was no one else in the room and nothing to see in the mirror but his own reflection. He shrugged his shoulders and picked up the mop. Then, turning to clean the floor, he recoiled in horror as he collided with a tall man who stood there with eyes that glowed blood-red. "W-w-what do you w-w-want?" stammered the young man.

The vampire smiled, revealing his deadly fangs. His nostrils flared.

The young man tried to defend himself with the wooden handle. With lightning speed the vampire gripped his throat and with the other hand snapped the wooden mop-handle like a twig. Panic-stricken the young man tried to kick out at the deadly fiend. The vampire pulled the cleaner towards him, then violently pushed him away. The young man's head hit the plate-glass mirror which shattered into large pieces, the force of the blow knocking him unconscious. The vampire burrowed into his neck. After he had fed, he carried the body to a cubicle, put him inside, then closed the door and, reaching over, locked it from the inside. Then he brushed himself with his hand, smoothed down his hair, licked his lips and wiped his mouth with a large handkerchief.

Checking the coast was clear, he left and headed for the ballroom. He entered the darkened room. Standing at the back, he scanned the rows of people sitting silently listening to Doctor Drachler. Some were even scribbling notes in the dim light. Several had small tape recorders.

"Surely the human body is more than recycled groceries," the Doctor continued.

The vampire moved up along the aisle and sat in a vacant seat at the side.

Frederika felt a sudden chill come over her. Some dark presence was in the room. She could feel it.

"The body and brain has an accumulation of experiences, a personality and some say possesses a soul. Many religions preach regeneration, rebirth and the promise of a spiritual life after this world. To conclude, the vampires, those creatures of darkness like ghosts and such ghouls, have been around in our imagination since early man first made a ghost of another by killing his kind. What is the dark allure of the vampire, nosferatu, vukodlak, upit or strigoi? Is it their mystery, forbidden passions, immortality, danger, power or romance that excites our imagination? Whatever it may be, it seems the vampire is alive and well in our popular culture thanks to such wonderful talents as Madame Frederika Kinski. Thank you." Doctor Drachler received a loud applause. Then the Secretary asked that the audience keep any questions they might have until Madame Kinski had finished her readings.

The Doctor sat beside Frederika. He could see she was tense. Her hands trembled. "Are you all right?" he asked.

"Yes . . . but I'm getting a very strange negative feeling from some member of the audience."

"They seem fine to me," he assured her.

"Perhaps I should take another sachet."

The vampire watched as the Doctor shielded Frederika while she drank something down from a silver beaker.

The Secretary again spoke glowingly about Madame Kinski and her many achievements and the awards she had received. "Will you please give a warm welcome to Madame Frederika Kinski, the world's leading novelist in the gothic genre." The audience clapped loudly. Frederika walked towards the lectern with her black leather folder.

"Good evening, how nice to be here!" she said. She took out a manuscript. "I would like to begin by reading something from my soon-to-be-published book The Dread of the Vampire." The vampire grinned to himself as he sat listening and watching the audience hang on her every word.

She began quietly. "Somewhere in the city a siren wailed. The old professor raised his eyes from the ancient scrolls and glanced towards the window. Beth, his cat, who was sleeping soundly, suddenly pulled herself into an alert position. Her fur bristled, she hissed at the door and scurried off to the bedroom. He looked puzzled, then returned to the scrolls. 'What a find,' he thought to himself. 'If these ancient writings are genuine then they give the precise time and location when evil first entered our world. These findings would explain so much, mankind would finally know that they have been and are still used as pawns by the Lord of the Underworld.' The clock struck midnight. The professor rubbed his tired eyes and yawned widely. He picked up the letter from his brother Saul and reread it. He had found the scrolls in a marketplace in Cairo in earthenware jars. Saul, a film maker, mainly of documentaries, was always on the look-out for bits and pieces for his scholarly elder brother to add to his collection of written antiquities. The professor was regarded as a world scholar on ancient languages. These scrolls were written in Aramaic, the language that Jesus himself spoke. The professor suddenly became aware of a foul odour, the stench assailing his nostrils. Behind the study door issued a strange hissing like that of a giant snake. The professor stood up, his body trembling. 'Who's there?' he called out. He moved slowly towards the door and reached for the handle. There was a sudden explosion and the door shot from its hinges. The professor was lifted clear off his feet and flung backwards by the force. He crashed against the wall, the door smashing into him, then slid down the wall, a deep gash on his forehead. He felt the blood course down his face. His hands fumbled for the glasses that had been knocked from his nose during the blast. He managed to locate them and returned them to his nose. One of the lenses was shattered. In the doorframe, grey-green smoke billowed up from the stairs. It soon cleared. There stood a tall man with flaccid skin and eyes that shone like burning coals. 'Who are you. What do you want?' the professor gasped. There was terror in his eyes. The creature smiled, revealing his deadly fangs. 'Professor Cohan,' the fiend glided towards him, 'Remember the proverb: curiosity killed the cat'. . ."

Frederika read excerpts from several of her novels. The crowd loved her mid-European accent which added to the richness of her expressive voice. She appeared relaxed but remained tense inside. She was totally convinced a dark force was in the ballroom. After she had finished her readings the Secretary invited the audience to ask questions.

The tall stranger stood up and stared hard at Frederika. "Madame Kinski, you seem so informed about the world of the undead, your writings would almost suggest a first-hand knowledge of vampires."

"Is that a question?" she responded.

He smiled. "I was wondering if you were a vampire yourself?" The audience laughed and applauded.

She paused, then spoke firmly. "When I write I believe totally in what I'm writing. If I did not, how could I expect my readers to believe? It's like a singer. There must be truth in the voice, otherwise you would not believe them if they sang about love, joy or sorrow." The audience applauded enthusiastically.

Another man raised his hand and stood up. "Madame Kinski, in your novel Dark Shadows . . ."

The vampire grinned wolfishly at Frederika, who was still watching him like a hawk, and briskly left the ballroom. There was a long pause as she watched him exit. Doctor Drachler tapped her lightly on the shoulder making her jump.

"Are you all right?" he enquired.

"Yes, please forgive me," she smiled, recovering herself and looking at the man who had asked the question. "Would you please repeat the question, sir?"

Doyler and Cooley hurried up the steps of the hotel. The vampire brushed past them, knocking Doyler down the steps.

"Watch it," Cooley shouted after him in annoyance. He helped Doyler to his feet.

"Don't fuss!" said Doyler. "I'm not an old woman."

"The bleedin' cheek! Isn't that the bloke we saw earlier?" Cooley stared after the stranger who seemed to vanish in front of his eyes.

"That's the Celtic Tiger for you," growled Doyler. "No respect, good manners gone out the door."

"He came out the door but I don't think he was big on good manners," grinned Cooley.

"It's a figure of speech," growled Doyler.

"I know! Let's get back inside before they're finished their talks," said Cooley.

"Wait," said Doyler. "Have you any Bisodol tablets? I've got fierce indigestion since I bolted down that supper."

"Here." Cooley produced a packet of antacid tablets. "You should keep a packet handy."

"Thanks," said Doyler, popping two of the tablets into his mouth. "I'll keep the packet."

When the evening talks were over and the book-signing completed, Inspector Wilson and Detective McGuire approached Madame Kinski and Doctor Drachler. They showed their police identification and introduced themselves.

"Was my talk an arresting experience?" she teased.

The two men smiled showing their appreciation of her humour.

"We enjoyed the talks very much," said Detective McGuire.

"Am I under arrest? I hardly think you two handsome gentlemen have come here looking for my autograph."

"How may we help you, gentlemen?" Doctor Drachler asked.

"May we find a quiet place to talk?" suggested Detective McGuire.

Cooley looked over at the two men talking to Madame Kinski and the Doctor. "They're two cops," he whispered out of the side of his mouth. "I can spot them a mile away."

Doyler watched them sit down in the lobby. "We can sit here and watch what's going on," he suggested.

"We're investigating a series of murders in the city," said Wilson gravely.

"Oh dear," said Frederika, "it's hard to imagine such a fair city having such horrible happenings."

"Sadly all big cities have their problems. What's unusual about these killings is that the victims are drained of blood."

Frederika gave a sideways glance towards the Doctor.

"How can we help?" asked the Doctor.

"Well," the Inspector paused, "this is going to sound

totally bizarre but, if we didn't know better, we would say these terrible crimes are the work of –"

"A vampire," Frederika finished for him.

"Well, yes, off the record of course," said McGuire. "That is, some crazy who thinks he may be a vampire. Or some religious cult which may be involved in some kind of weird blood-letting ritual."

"All my vampires are of the imagination," said Frederika.

"Yes, of course," said the Inspector, "but you both have a vast wealth of knowledge and experience of the subject."

"Now you flatter us," she retorted.

"Madame Kinski, any help you can give us to track down this vicious killer would be of immense help. For in all our years of police work we have never come across anything like this." There was an edge to his voice.

Frederika stared at the Inspector. "I will be glad to tell you all I know."

"Let us pretend for the moment that vampires do exist," said Wilson.

"They do exist," said the Doctor gravely. "I would not normally profess my beliefs so openly. I do so only because of the sincerity of your requests."

Wilson glanced at McGuire.

"Allow me, Alex," said Frederika. "Vampires are known as the 'undead'. They are predators who prey on humans to feed their great hunger which can only be sated by warm blood. Some vampires were human like you or me but were attacked by a vampire and, if they did not die, became vampires themselves."

"So you believe those poor murdered victims could now be vampires out searching for human blood?" said McGuire.

"No," replied the Doctor. "The vampire in question is probably too clever for that. It kills its victims in the attacks. It doesn't want vampires wandering all over the city competing for blood. Besides, it would put him at risk."

"How put him at risk?" asked McGuire.

"Well, if there was a plague of vampires the authorities would soon be wise to it and would find them out and destroy them. This way he can move about like a shadow leaving some dead but not causing a national panic."

"Victims only become vampires if the vampire mixes his own blood with the person he chooses to initiate," said Frederika.

"How else do people become vampires then?" the Inspector asked.

"As we discussed in our talk," said Drachler, "people dabbling in the dark arts, murderers when executed and people who commit suicide may return as vampires. These, of course, are the stuff of legends."

"Vampires seem to have been on the earth as long as humans have," added Frederika.

"How does one destroy a vampire?" the Inspector asked.

"A stake through the heart like in the movies?" suggested McGuire.

"Yes," said Frederika, "just like in the movies."

"It is recommended you cut off the head and stuff the mouth with garlic cloves," the Doctor added.

"Charming," sighed the Inspector. "What about bullets, knives?"

"The vampire has surprisingly good healing powers therefore bullets are useless against him. The knife must be aimed at the heart, then the neck severed."

"They have the strength of ten men," said Frederika. "Contrary to popular belief, they can walk out in the daylight but usually avoid direct sunlight."

"Even your celebrated author Bram Stoker, who wrote the chilling Dracula novel knew this," Doctor Drachler added.

"Where do they go to sleep?"

"Anywhere," replied the Doctor. "It is said they must have some soil from their native land to rest upon. This need be no more than, say, the size of a bagful of sugar. They can sleep for years, centuries even. Normally they will sleep twenty days a month. Yet some will just rest from sunrise to sunset."

"It depends on the individual nosferatu," said Frederika.

"And what defence is there against them?" asked Wilson.

"The sacred host will protect one, also the crucifix, and holy water can be sprinkled on your clothes as a defence. The vampire cannot stand the smell of garlic. Yet there are some vampires who are very cunning and have learned ways to get around these defences."

"Well, thank you. We won't take up any more of your time," said Inspector Wilson.

"We can see they're still lining up for your autograph," smiled McGuire.

"May we have a contact number?" added Wilson.

The Doctor produced a fountainpen and wrote two numbers on the back of his card then handed it to McGuire. The policeman thanked them again and left.

"You're right," said Doyler. "They look like the law all right." He looked around at the people, some holding books, waiting to get them signed by Madame Kinksi, others in deep conversation. He smiled broadly. "They look surprisingly normal for a bunch of vampire lovers."

"Horses for courses," said Cooley.

"Why don't they have evenings talking about cowboy movies? Now that would be interesting."

"I agree," said Cooley. "I'm sure you'd gets loads of Western fans."

"John Wayne is still as popular as ever despite the fact that he's dead all these years," said Doyler.

"Ah you can't keep a good cowboy down," laughed Cooley.

"What's the fascination with all this spooky stuff?" sighed Doyler.

A man carrying a bunch of leaflets approached them.

"Good evening, gentlemen. Were you at the talks?"

"Oh yes, very interesting," said Doyler.

The man handed them some of the leaflets. "There is a Dracula convention taking place in London in September. There are some excellent speakers coming. We are hoping to have Christopher Lee as the guest speaker at the Dracula dinner."

"Oh, I've always admired him," said Cooley. "He's still my favourite actor to play Dracula."

"I agree," said the man. "Would you please pass some of these leaflets to your colleagues?"

"Oh yes, to be sure," said Doyler. As the man walked away Doyler whispered to Cooley, "Would he ever get a life!" He yawned. "I'm ready for me bed. The thought of driving out to Wicklow doesn't exactly please me."

"I'll do it," said Cooley. "Why don't you head home!"

"Well, I'd love to, but I want to find out what we're supposed to be doing for the Doctor and his ladyfriend." He winked at Cooley. "I also hope to get a few quid out of him before the night's out."

They left the hotel after midnight. Doctor Drachler told Doyler and Cooley he would not be needing them over the next few days but would require their services at the weekend.

"That's fine, Doctor," said Doyler, "but as you can imagine we have incurred some expenses since you and the good lady Madame Kinski arrived."

The Doctor turned to check on Frederika who was still being detained by enthusiastic fans. He then took out his calf-leather wallet and handed them one hundred and fifty pounds each.

"Thank you, Doctor. That should cover our costs."

"We can talk about your fees when you have completed your assignments."

"We'll talk soon. It's always a pleasure doing business with you," Doyler smiled.

"Thank you, Doctor Drachler," said Cooley as he pushed his half of the money into a shabby cloth wallet.

"Come, Frederika," said the Doctor, rescuing her from her adoring fans.

Drachler and Frederika drove in silence for a long time. There were patches of fog as they left the city. The Doctor gave a sigh. "I'm glad that one's over. Still, they were a wonderful audience. Very attentive, and the questions were very intelligent." Frederika didn't respond. She was looking out into the darkness.

"Are you very tired?" asked Drachler. "You must be! Rest and I'll wake you when we've arrived back at the manor."

"He was there," she spoke quietly.

"Who?" the Doctor enquired.

"Baron Rellick," she answered as if in a trance.

"You're not serious!" he exclaimed in shock.

"I am. Even in the darkened room I knew it was he. I sensed his vile presence."

"But you haven't seen him since you were a child."

"I could never forget his face," she said darkly. "The one that caused my family so much misery."

"Do you want to talk about it?" he asked softly.

"No, not now." She rested her head on the Doctor's shoulder. "Dear Alex, you are the best thing that happened to me since I lost my family. You've filled a great void."

"It is you, Frederika, who have brought me such happiness. I, who never gave myself up to anything but the fanatical pursuit of my interests. I have never been close to anyone until I met you."

Frederika smiled and gave a gentle laugh. "You remember the first day we met in that museum in Bombay?"

He laughed loudly. "How could I forget? I was so busy staring at that wonderful statue of Lord Krishna that I backed into you, nearly knocking you against a glass case."

"Then, as you apologised, you stepped on my foot!" she teased.

"Oh dear, don't remind me. I was so clumsy . . . it's embarrassing to recall."

"You offered to make it up to me by buying me dinner," said Frederika.

"Yes," he smiled. "Then at dinner the penny dropped. I realised that you were the famous novelist of the occult. Here we are, two years later, growing closer all the time. That reminds me of Robert Browning and his beloved Elizabeth, and his poem which begins, 'Grow old along with me, the best is yet to be'." He smiled. "Of course, I'm years older than you. I'm what people would call a 'sugar daddy'." He grinned.

"Are you so sure?" she said softly.

"About what?" he asked.

"That you are years older than me?" she asked, raising her head to look at him.

"Now you are teasing," he smiled. "We only have to look in the mirrors. People think I am your father, perhaps even your grandfather."

She rested her head on his shoulder again and closed her eyes.

"We're very near now," he said tenderly. Then to his amazement he could see a very bright light beyond the woods. "Look!" he said in a puzzled voice.

She opened her eyes. "What is it?"

"I don't know!"

As they drove down the narrow road and got beyond the woods they could see all. To their horror, the lovely house they were renting was ablaze. The flame was spreading to the surrounding area, setting some of the trees on fire. They pulled the car to an abrupt stop.

"Oh no, I can't believe it," Frederika cried.

A man seemed to come from nowhere and tapped on the glass, startling them both. Frederika shrieked.

"Sorry for alarming you like this," he panted, "but I live just up the road in the small cottage. I was coming home from the Goat's Head when I spotted the house on fire. I've phoned the fire brigade. They should be here soon."

Frederika got out of the car and walked towards the fire. The Doctor hurried after her and forced her back. She turned to him and sobbed, "This is terrible, horrible."

He tried to comfort her. "We will head back to Dublin and you can stay in the Shelbourne Hotel. You liked it there."

She pulled away and cupped his face in her hands. "You don't understand. My medicine has been destroyed too. Have you any idea what that means?"

"Surely we can get some more," he assured her.

"No, we cannot. He's done this! I know it!" She stared back at the house.

"You don't mean –"

"Yes, I do. This is the work of Baron Rellick. He wants to destroy my life! He has tried it before in Rome, Paris, London, anywhere I've settled and now he's doing it again. Only I didn't think he would try it so quickly. And you, dear Alex, you must leave Ireland tomorrow – you are in mortal danger."

"I'm not afraid of this Baron Rellick. I've confronted a similar fiend before."

"It is I you should be afraid of," she said sorrowfully.

"I don't understand."

The fire brigade's siren pierced the night's silence.

# Chapter 7

Doctor Drachler headed up the stairs to Frederika's room the next morning. He had managed to get her a suite in the Shelbourne Hotel despite the fact he was told the hotel was completely full. When he explained it was the famous Madame Kinski who had stayed earlier in the week they immediately found her the finest suite in the hotel. 'The power of a name,' he mused.

He stood anxiously outside her room before knocking, afraid that she might be still asleep. She had not been well the night before when he brought her here. The shock of the fire had deeply affected her. He knocked gently. There was no response. He knocked again, a little more firmly this time and called her name. The door opened.

She was in her dressing gown but seemed bright and alert.

"Dear Alex!" She kissed him on the cheek, held his hand and led him into the room. "Coffee?" she asked.

"Yes, please."

"As you can see I was expecting you. Breakfast for two delivered several minutes ago."

"Perfect timing," he smiled, removing his overcoat and silk scarf. They sat in silence. He watched her pour the coffee, and butter a hot croissant for him. "How are you feeling?" he enquired tenderly. She produced two sachets of her powder and smiled.

"I found them in my purse, my emergency supply. I've enough to get me through the week. God knows what will happen after that."

He sipped his coffee and looked at her.

"Dear Alex, you have been so kind and considerate to me ever since we first met."

He smiled.

"It is time you knew the truth about me . . . this is not easy for me . . ." She sighed.

"If you don't want to –" he interjected.

"But I do," she insisted. "It happened when we were holidaying in Venice, my family and I. I was only eight at the time. It was New Year's Eve. I remember there was the most glorious fireworks display. A stranger who was staying at our hotel came up to us. He introduced himself as Baron Rellick and explained he had seen us in the hotel and that he would be honoured if we would join him for supper. My father thanked him but said that the little one, that was me, needed rest. My mother was taken with the handsome

Baron and insisted we go. By all accounts we had a splendid supper. My father as usual drank too much. I fell asleep in my mother's arms. The following day I awoke to find I had two puncture-marks on my neck. My mother was clutching me tightly. She too had the deadly wounds on her beautiful neck. When I enquired where Papa was she said sadly that he had gone to the angels. She sobbed and sobbed. Several days later a stern-looking priest examined our wounds. He said something to my mother which made her cry out. They would have to visit the tomb where Papa was laid to rest. My mother reluctantly agreed. The priest said there might be some hope for us . . ." Frederika sobbed. The Doctor held her hand. She continued. "The Baron came for my mother the following night, drained her of her precious blood and when the doctor arrived she was dead. The priest came and told me my mother had gone to join my father in Heaven. The following day was the funeral. My aunt and her husband came for me, but not before the priest insisted that we visit a monastery in Luppiano outside Florence. It was a long and very tiring journey. I was told I had the fever and must rest. When I did sleep I had the most horrible nightmares. In the monastery of St Mark I remember a kind old monk checking my eyes and my neck, then in the evening giving me some medicine. 'Drink it, my child,' he insisted. His voice was warm and comforting. It was this medicine that saved my life and sustained me and kept me from becoming . . ."

"A vampire," he finished her sentence.

"Yes, a vampire!"

"Good Lord," he recoiled.

"Now you know, dear Alex. Now you will hate me for keeping this dark secret from you for so long," she said sadly.

"No, no, dear Frederika. On the contrary! I've always dreamed of tracking down a real vampire and perhaps convincing it to change its ways."

"It!" she retorted.

"I mean, asking him or her to reveal their secrets, to write a book, appear on television and radio. Explain to the world the dark side of life and to warn mankind that pure evil does exist! I know it sounds crazy –"

"If you want me to, I will go on television and explain that I am a vampire."

"My dear Frederika, forgive me! I am a selfish beast, always caught up in my obsessions! I did not mean you. I know there is not a drop of evil in you."

"Perhaps there is," she said darkly.

"When did this terrible thing happen to you?" he asked.

"Eighteen seventy-nine."

"Eighteen seventy-nine," he repeated in total disbelief.

"Less than two hours into the New Year."

A loud knock on the door startled Frederika.

"Who could that be?" the Doctor wondered. "Perhaps room service."

The Doctor opened the door. There stood Inspector Wilson and Detective McGuire. "Inspector Wilson," said the Doctor.

"Good morning," he said sharply, "may we have a word with yourself and Madame Kinski?"

"Show the gentlemen in," said Frederika. "Good detective work to track us here so quickly. Do sit down"

"Thank you. We are here on police business," said McGuire.

"You obviously haven't come to join me for breakfast," she smiled.

"Look at this." He produced a copy of the Irish Independent.

The Doctor took the paper from him. The headline read: Vampire-Style Killing Takes Place At Vampire Conference. Drachler read aloud: "The Gresham Hotel was the scene of the grisly murder of a young Spanish cleaner which took place at a Vampire Night. World-famous Polish horror writer Madame Frederika Kinski and vampire expert Doctor Drachler . . ." The Doctor stopped and glanced at Frederika.

"Are we suspects, Inspector?" asked Frederika.

The Inspector did not respond. He nodded to McGuire.

"What time was it when you left the hotel last night?" asked McGuire.

Drachler was responding when McGuire's mobile rang.

It was the forensic department calling. McGuire listened intently. "Thank you, good work." He turned to the Inspector.

"Well, what is it?" Wilson asked gruffly.

"It seems the killing took place at around nine thirty – during the talks."

The Inspector took a deep breath. "If there's coffee in the pot we'll have some."

"Certainly," said Frederika, reaching for two fresh cups on a nearby tray.

There was silence as she poured.

Wilson put several spoons of sugar in his coffee, stirred it and then looked up. "Well, that lets you two off the hook."

"Well, that's a relief," the Doctor retorted.

"You see, Madame Kinski," McGuire added, "we were there throughout the talks and had both of you in view all the time."

"We still need to question you on your movements however. And perhaps there may have been something you observed during the talks that might help us. Did you notice anything odd, unusual? Anyone behaving in a suspicious way? Did anyone leave the ballroom during the talks, for instance?" He waited for them to respond, his eyes intent.

"Inspector . . ." Frederika began.

They waited.

She looked helplessly at Drachler. He took her hand and nodded.

"I know who the killer is," she said.

The two policeman stared in amazement.

"The person you seek is a man called Baron Rellick."

McGuire whipped out a notebook and scribbled the name in it.

"I have been tracking this fiend across Europe. He murdered my parents."

"This man is no mortal," said the Doctor. "This Baron Rellick is a genuine vampire!"

# Chapter 8

"I thought he didn't need us until the weekend," Doyler grumbled. "We'll have to cancel that furniture job."

"Listen, I'll get my brother and his mates to deliver the furniture to the auction rooms," Cooley offered.

"I suppose it's the best thing," said Doyler. "Only tell them we're on a commission – thirty percent of what they get."

"Don't worry," said Cooley. "Packie will look after us."

"Let's have a cup of tea before we head out," said Doyler.

"Okay, I'll make it," said Cooley, heading for the kitchen.

Doyler picked up the paper. "And make us a cheese sandwich," he shouted to Cooley. He began to read. "Good Lord!" he exclaimed.

"What's up?" asked Cooley, popping his head around the door frame.

"Remember when we were at the hotel last night? Well, some poor bloke was killed in the toilet. There were holes in his neck and his body was drained of blood."

"You're not serious," said Cooley, coming to look at the paper

"It's here in black and white," Doyler declared.

"Don't tell me there's a bloomin' vampire stalking the city!"

"I hope Madame Kinski has nothing to do with this," sighed Doyler. "I've a bad feeling she may be involved. It does seem very peculiar that she should arrive in Dublin, a vampire expert, then some poor bloke clocks out and is drained of blood, in a hotel she's lecturing in." Suddenly he jumped up, rushed over to a chest of drawers and began frantically to rummage among the clothes.

"What are you at?" Cooley wondered.

"Make the tea! I'll show you in a minute if I find it."

When Cooley arrived with the two mugs of tea and several cheese sandwiches, Doyler held a crucifix up to him.

"Put the cross away! I'm not Dracula," Cooley chuckled.

"You may laugh but this cross belonged to my mother, the Lord rest her poor soul. It's going into my pocket for our protection, just in case we meet one of those bloodsuckers, even if it is Madame Kinski!"

The Doctor sat on a bench in St Stephen's Green looking

at the ducks. Frederika was being interviewed by some newspaper. The Doctor had warned her to talk about nothing but her books.

He noticed Cooley and Doyler hurrying up the pathway.

Doyler was panting. "Sorry we're late. This city is choking with traffic."

"Gridlock," added Cooley, "that's what it is."

"Indeed," said the Doctor. "Gentlemen," he said solemnly, "Madame Kinski is in a terrible dilemma. Her medicine has almost run out and she cannot get any more until she gets back to Budapest. The prescription was stolen from her while she was in Paris a few months ago."

"Why can't she go to the chemist or ask a doctor to write her one?" Cooley suggested.

"It is not that simple," he snapped. "This prescription is a nineteenth-century document. It's irreplaceable. The monk who wrote the prescription was killed by a vampire, together with his fellow monks. The monastery was razed to the ground. Fortunately this secret prescription was copied a day earlier and given to Frederika's uncle."

"I'm completely lost, Doctor," said Doyler. "What's the matter with Madame Kinski that she can't get an ordinary prescription from a doctor?"

"You see, Madame Kinski has a rare blood disorder and must take this medicine in order to survive. The medicine cannot be made without the formula. The formula was stolen in Paris by a Baron Rellick. We believe he is now in

Dublin and most certainly will have the document with him. Indeed, on his person – it is so precious he would not let it out of his sight."

"This Baron – Rellick," said Cooley, "he wouldn't have anything to do with the killing last evening, would he?"

The Doctor stared from one to the other. "I believe he has," he said gravely. "He was there. Frederika saw him."

"Don't tell me you think he's a vampire?" said Doyler.

"I do," he replied.

"Well, Doctor Drachler, we'd love to help you but if I follow your drift you want us to locate this Baron vampire. And get the prescription from him?"

"Exactly!" the Doctor responded.

Doyler laughed nervously. "Well, we have to think of our own health first. We don't want to put ourselves in harm's way. No offence."

"I will pay you well if you can recover this prescription for me."

"How much?" asked Cooley.

"A thousand pounds."

"Each?" asked Doyler.

"Yes! But I must have it before the weekend. It's a matter of life and death."

"Excuse me, Doctor," said Cooley, "but where are we supposed to begin to search for this Baron?"

"I have no idea," he sighed. "All I know is he's tall, dark, striking-looking and very dangerous."

"That's a great help," Doyler mumbled to himself.

"Wait a minute," said Cooley. "Maybe he's that weird-looking fellow who knocked you down on the steps, Doyler!"

Doyler started. "Yeah! That must have been him! Fits the description."

"So at least we know what he looks like!"

"Maybe," said Doyler. "If that was him. But I bet it was."

"Good. That's a start," said Drachler. "I will, of course, be making my own enquiries." He stood up. "I must go. We must keep in contact. If I discover anything about his whereabouts I will phone you. Please take the utmost care. Remember he really is a vampire. And carry a crucifix at all times."

They watched him walk away.

Then he stopped and turned back to them. "Frederika is my life. Please help her. There will be a bonus on top of what we've agreed if you can find it quickly. Please do your very best."

"I don't know about you but I could do with another cup of tea," said Doyler.

They left the park and walked over to a small café nearby. There they began to puzzle out where a vampire might be hiding. They decided the most likely place would be a cemetery. They ate lots of cakes, drank several cups of tea and wrote down as many cemeteries as they could think of in the Dublin area.

Cooley scratched his chin, then pulled at the lobe of his ear.

Doyler picked his nose, then rubbed his hand back and forwards across his mouth several times. He gave out a loud sigh. "This is an impossible task. It's like looking for a needle in a haystack."

"Or a hen's tooth," Cooley sniggered.

Doyler laughed loudly. "Madness!" he sighed. "And we don't even know if he's still in Dublin."

"Maybe he's staying at the Gresham!" said Cooley and then his expression changed.

"What's up with you?" Doyler asked.

"Is your name Doyle?" asked a stern voice from behind. Doyler swivelled in his chair to see two tall men standing there.

"Who's enquiring?" he replied. Cooley kicked him under the table.

"I am Inspector Wilson and this is Detective McGuire. We're investigating several recent murders in the city."

"What's that to do with us?" Doyler retorted anxiously.

The two policemen sat down.

"You were at a talk last evening in the Gresham Hotel," said the Inspector.

"Yes," said Cooley, "along with over two hundred other people."

"How well do you know this Madame Kinski?" McGuire probed.

"Who said we knew her?" Doyler responded.

"You were seen with a Doctor Drachler in the Green."

Doyler fingered his shirt collar. The idea of being spied on made him very uncomfortable. He emptied his cup and poured himself some more. "OK, we know Doctor Drachler and we had dealings with Madame Kinski."

"What kind of dealings?" McGuire asked.

"We chauffeur her and the Doctor about," said Cooley. "Things like that."

"Did you notice anything unusual while attending the talks in the hotel?" Wilson asked.

"We noticed a lot of sad people into creepy stuff. Get a life, that's what I say," Doyler smirked.

Cooley lit up a cigarette.

"You're at a non-smoking table," said McGuire.

"Oh yeah!" He grinned nervously, then stubbed out the cigarette on his saucer.

"You have something to add?" McGuire looked sharply at Cooley.

"Well, we didn't stay for all the talks. We slipped away for something to eat. But on the way out and coming back in to the hotel we passed this man."

"Go on," insisted the Inspector.

"This man knocked Doyler off his feet and as you can see he's no waif."

"Describe him," said McGuire, whipping out a notebook and pen..

"I'd say he was a foreigner and a bit of a dandy," said Doyler.

"He was tall, very slim, good features, black wavy hair. But there was an air of menace about him. Not the kind of fellow you'd like to get on the wrong side of."

"I'd agree with that!" Doyler added.

"His clothes were fancy, long black coat, a bit old-fashioned, like someone you'd see in one of those Victorian plays on the BBC," Cooley offered. "Of course, there were others at that talk dressed rather strangely. I think they call them Goths. It's a kind of fashion."

"Chief," said McGuire, "let's go back and check the tape from the hotel's surveillance camera again – it might have recorded that incident."

"You're right, Detective. Let's go."

Wilson and McGuire hurried back to the station where they sat and watched the footage of the previous evening at the Gresham again, the operator spooling the tapes backwards and forwards until they saw Doyler and Cooley leaving.

"Stop it there," McGuire insisted. "Replay! Freeze!"

Wilson and McGuire couldn't believe their eyes. They could clearly see Doyler and Cooley leaving the hotel and reacting to someone at the front door of the hotel. But no one could be seen. "Fast forward to where these two men arrive back into the lobby!" The operator did as requested. They could see Doyler being knocked off his feet and Cooley reacting. But where the mysterious stranger should be, there was nothing only the background.

"What do you make of that?" asked McGuire.

"Weird!" said the Inspector grimly. "Very weird indeed!"

# Chapter 9

Dublin, September 1897

Professor Boam walked down the wooden gangplank of the schooner. He was a tall very pale man with a grey beard. He was a man on a mission. A heavy grey fog surrounded the Dublin port.

"The fog sure is not confined to London," he quipped to Captain Marsh.

The captain, a jolly red-faced heavy-set man laughed and nodded in agreement. Out of the darkness a slim young man appeared. The professor stared intently at him.

"Professor Boam?" the young man addressed him.

He nodded.

"Charles Howard. You are welcome, sir. May I take your bag?"

The professor handed it to him but held on to his small brown leather case.

"The cab is waiting just over here."

"A good trip, professor?" he enquired, breaking the silence as they journeyed into the city.

"I'm bone-tired and hungry," the professor answered.

Charles Howard was the son of a clergyman, a one-time friend of the professor's who was now dead from a cholera outbreak ten years earlier.

Young Howard had arranged supper in a popular eating house called The Raven's Wing along the quays. He had booked a private room in the back so that they would not be disturbed. As they entered this room in The Raven's Wing two other men were seated at the table, one drinking port, the other porter. They immediately stood to attention at the appearance of Professor Boam. They noticed that the old professor had a limp and the cane that he used was not a normal one. They suspected it was a cane sword. Howard formally introduced the professor. They greeted each other.

After they ordered food, the professor thanked them for meeting him. He explained his journey had taken him across most of Europe over the past three months. They were all familiar with his work. They too had vowed to work in the service of the light and to rid the world of the curse of vampirism.

"Gentlemen," he spoke gravely as he drank some brandy and port. "I have killed seven vampires in the past three months. Four men, two women and a boy no more than fourteen years of age. I have lost two of my most loyal and trusted friends, killed in the line of duty by that burning black-hearted fiend Baron Rellick. He somehow manages always to stay one step ahead of me. He knows I am after him; he seems to enjoy the fun of the chase. It is like a game of chess for him. But gentlemen, he will not escape me this time. That I promise." He emptied his glass and ordered another drink. His voice mellowed. "Fortunately I've been financed by an angel of light by the name of Madame Kinski. She too has suffered at the hands of this dark fiend. Her parents were killed by this monster while she was a child. Then he struck again last year, killing her husband."

"That's terrible," Howard responded.

"Indeed it was – they were only married a year. He was one of the finest restorers of paintings in Italy, perhaps Europe. I was called by Cardinal Vincento and a friend of Madame Kinski who was familiar with my work. Now, gentlemen, although you have all agreed to offer your services for free, I am now in the agreeable position to be able to offer you payment."

"No there is no need," the men protested.

"Gentlemen, the labourer is worthy of his hire." He handed them a sum of money each. "Don't see it as blood money," he joked. "Now what news have you for me, gentlemen?"

"We have been checking the ports for the past three days and nights, as you suggested in your telegram. Last evening a tall stranger in a black cape arrived in Kingstown from Holyhead. My brother Pat followed at a safe distance. He arrived in the city by hansom cab, Pat was right behind. He followed him up the quays but somehow lost him at Church Street. My brother said he seemed to disappear in front of his eyes like a puff of smoke. I checked with the boat he arrived on. The captain said he remembered the man. 'A most arrogant man,' he concluded, 'although he seemed to tip well.' The strange thing was that one of his crew had gone missing. Thought he might have fallen overboard."

"He has fed on that crew member, I'm convinced," sighed the professor. "So he will not need to hunt for days – perhaps weeks. I thought I had tracked him down in London. He certainly had killed at least two people over the three days he was there. The police recovered a body in the Fulham area two weeks ago near an old warehouse. I hurried there and found his resting place in the basement of the premises but he was gone. I placed a crucifix in his coffin so he could not return. That evening he attacked my two colleagues and slew them, leaving a bloodstained note for me. I knew the menace would leave England. I just had a hunch he would come here. My hunch seems to have paid off. Gentlemen, you know your city. Where your brother lost sight of this fiend – is there an old cemetery?"

The men looked at each other.

"Well, yes, there's Saint Michan's church – it's on Church Street."

"Of course," the other man said enthusiastically. "There is a graveyard there and there are crypts below the church."

The professor's eyes widened. "Tell me all you know."

"Go on, Richard. You're the Trinity College student," said Howard.

The young man cleared his throat. "The church is just down from Inn's Quay in Church Street. The original church was built circa 1095. The name Michan is supposed to come from an old Danish saint. The vaults are rather unique. There are mummified bodies in a remarkable state of preservation. One is said to be of a knight of the crusades –"

"Gentlemen," the professor cut off the young man in mid-sentence, "thanks to your good work I believe we have located the vampire's resting place. Saint Michan's," he said looking skywards. Then turning to the young man, "I believe this Baron Rellick would fancy the idea of resting in such an historical place. It would appeal to his ego. I will rest now. We shall meet before sunset tomorrow. Wear protection, come armed with crucifixes and bring holy water. I'll carry the sacred host – I have permission from the Cardinal of Milan to take some in my quest to root out these evil fiends . . . these nosferatus!"

It was a bitterly cold night when they met near the Four Courts. Two of the men carried tar-sticks to light their way. The professor carried wooden stakes and a mallet, a small revolver and his cane sword. Visibility was poor because of a freezing fog that had descended like a shroud over the city. All the men were on time; it was the professor who arrived half an hour late. The men were blowing on their hands to keep warm. "Good to see you all," he said. "I have been around the church and the cemetery earlier this morning. We may have to break the lock to get down to the crypt. Hopefully it will not be necessary. I think we should catch the fiend as he leaves his lair."

"The idea of his resting below a church that still is a place of worship seems very strange," Howard remarked.

"That's the kind of thing that would amuse this conceited vampire." The professor took out a hip flash and offered it around. The young men declined. The professor took a swig of rum from the silver flask. "Wonderful for keeping out the chill," he explained.

They were now huddled about close to Saint Michan's. They watched the street lamps being lit up. They kept a silent vigil, shivering from cold and fear.

The professor sensed this. "Gentlemen. Be brave, be strong. You are doing the will of God. Wait until I make the first move. If I fall victim to the bloodsucker, it's up to you – you must drive a stake into my heart and cut my head off." The men recoiled in horror. "For friendship's sake I demand this of you." Then he smiled. "Never fear. I don't intend to fall victim to this brute."

Their vigil was long and cold. They began to wonder if

they had made a mistake regarding the vampire's resting place. The sound of a horse's hooves broke the silence. The lanterns on the carriage were like two flaming eyes piercing the thick fog. They heard muffled voices as the cab came to a halt. A young woman thanked the driver, pulled her shawl over her head and hurried home. The cab driver turned the horse and the cab headed off slowly towards the quays.

Then a scream pierced the night. The men looked at each other in horror, then moved quickly in the direction of the scream. As they got closer they could see a black form stooped over the woman who was lying on the footpath. The professor released his sword from its wooden sheath and ran at the vampire who was busy draining her of her blood. The vampire turned and hissed, blood dripping from his mouth. With lightning speed the professor ran his sword through him. He gave out an unearthly shriek and fell back on the black railings. The other men hurried to help, some checking on the young woman, the others holding up crucifixes to ward off the monster. The vampire snarled and pulled the sword from his chest. The professor hurried to open his bag and pulled out a revolver and a cross. The Baron lashed out at the young men, knocking both to the ground, piercing one through the shoulder with the sword. The other two men jumped on the vampire and tried to pin him down. But he proved too strong for them even in his weakened state.

"Hold him," the professor demanded as he aimed a shot, hitting the vampire on the shoulder.

They could not hold him. He escaped, the professor in hot pursuit. The vampire climbed the railings of Saint Michan's and leaped from the top to the ground as the professor scrambled up on the locked gates and tried to climb over. Two of the other men were climbing up the railings.

"I'll get you, you devil," shouted the professor as he neared the top of the gates.

The vampire turned to see the young men clearing the railings. The professor dropped to the ground, then staggered to his feet. The Baron rushed at him, knocking him with great force against the railings. As the professor held out a crucifix, the vampire stabbed him in the wrist with his own sword-cane, making him drop the cross.

The vampire grinned a devilish grin. "You may have scotched the serpent, but you have not killed it."

"Roast in hell, fiend!" the professor yelled.

"You first," the vampire sniggered slyly and thrust the sword into the professor's heart.

The young men cried out.

The vampire stood as the young men surrounded him.

"We have you now," said Howard.

"Are you so sure?" the Baron grinned. In front of their very eyes he turned into a green mist. The men couldn't believe what they were seeing. The green vapour streamed snake-like through the iron doors that led down into the crypt.

They hurried over to the professor, but he was dead. The young woman too lay dead.

"We'll have to get you to a doctor," Howard said to one of the young men who was bleeding badly from his wounds. "But first we must finish the task for the sake of the professor."

Two of them agreed to go down into the crypt. They lit the torches and broke the lock on the iron doors. Lifting one of the doors up, they could see steps that led downwards. The air felt dry. The two men held crosses out in front of them. Their hearts pounded as they entered, not knowing whether the vampire was lurking in the darkness, waiting for them. Large cobwebs hung from the ceiling on the left. There were coffins stacked on top of each other. The mummified bodies of the so-called Vikings could be seen, and several other bodies lay about in broken coffins.

A rat scurried past them, causing them to panic. To the right there were several wooden coffins. In the corner below the others was an ebony coffin. They knew it must belong to the Baron for it was too new-looking and was carefully placed on two stone blocks. There was a locked gate at the entrance. They tried to break the lock. As they hammered at it with the handle of the pistol, rats began to appear from every direction. Soon there were hundreds of black rats scurrying about.

"Let's get out of here," one of the young men panicked and ran up the steps into the cold night. He began to take deep breaths. "Come on, Howard," he shouted down the passageway. The rats were running over his shoes, some leaping up at him. One even ran up the leg of his trousers. He screamed, pulled out a penknife and ripped open the trouser leg. The rat made a quick exit.

Sweat was pouring down his face. The floor of the crypt seemed alive with the twisting and writhing bodies of the sewer rats. Howard took a sacred wafer from a silver container that was in the professor's bag. He reached as far as he could through the metal bars and tossed it onto the black coffin. Then he tied several crucifixes onto the iron bars with some twine.

"That should keep this fiend trapped down here, if he's not already destroyed." He had seen the professor run it through with his sword and also hit him with a well-aimed shot from his pistol. He wanted to set the place on fire, but for the sake of the beautiful church he refrained. He hurried down the passageway, then up the steps and closed the iron door, pushing the bolt across to secure it.

"Are you all right?" the other man enquired.

"Yes, I have sealed that devil in his coffin – hopefully the rats will find him."

They broke the lock on the gates and carried the body of the professor outside, only to be confronted by two policemen.

"What's going on here?" one asked sternly. The other constable blew his whistle.

# Chapter 10

"No, Doctor, I'm sorry. Still no news. I am aware of how urgent it is. Yes, we'll call to the hotel at nine o'clock. Yes, Doctor, to be sure." Doyler put down the phone.

"You don't have to tell me who that was," said Cooley, pouring them both a mug of tea.

Doyler paced up and down the room. "He seems totally stressed out – the Doctor."

"Well, he's worried about his beloved Frederika," said Cooley. The phone rang again.

"I hope it's not him again," sighed Doyler.

"Maybe it's the law," Cooley teased.

"Don't you start." Doyler pointed his finger in mock annoyance. He picked up the phone. "Hello," he said gruffly. "Oh Martin, how's it going?" He turned to Cooley. "It's your cousin Martin."

Cooley hurried to the phone. "Well, have you any news? You have? I hope it's good!"

Doyler chewed on a fig-roll biscuit and watched Cooley's facial expressions. He could tell a lot about his friend from his face. He could see Cooley's mouth widen to a big grin. "Good on ye," said Cooley. "Thanks a million!" He put down the phone. He then sat down, carefully put lots of milk and two heaped teaspoons of sugar into his tea, stirred it and picked up a biscuit.

"Well, are you going to keep me in suspense all day?" snapped Doyler.

"Finish up your tea," said Cooley. "We have an important meeting with my cousin Martin and Billy Roche."

"Who's he?" asked Doyler.

"All will be revealed," said Cooley. He drank back his tea and shoved the biscuit in his mouth, pulled on his jacket and headed for the door. Then, turning back he yelled, "Are you coming?"

Doyler gulped down his tea and followed after him.

Cooley had arranged to meet Martin and Billy at the Winding Stairs, a Georgian building overlooking the Ha'penny bridge. The Winding Stairs was a bookshop with cafés on the first and second floor.

"Ah, this is a grand spot," said Doyler smiling at the pretty waitress. "How come we haven't been here before?"

"I dunno – we've been in nearly every other cafe in Dublin. Ah, there they are!"

His cousin was coming up the stairs followed by an elderly gentleman with wisps of grey hair protruding from his tightly fitting woollen peaked cap. The man was small and slight with a bushy grey moustache. He was very bow-legged. His whole appearance was comical-looking, almost like a caricature of himself.

Doyler grinned as Martin introduced Billy Roche. The man had a strong handshake for such a thin, frail-looking person. They sat by the window. Roche looked out the window at the Ha'penny Bridge which was being restored to its former glory. "It's a terrible pity they never built that art gallery across the Liffey. That would have been sensational." Doyler and Cooley looked blank. "You know, the one proposed by Lord Alfred Beit? An artist's impression of the design can be seen in the Municipal Gallery."

"Oh fascinating," said Doyler.

"This man has forgotten more about Dublin than I know," said Martin, patting Billy on the back.

"Well, I hope he hasn't forgotten what we're anxious to know," said Doyler laughing.

"Let's order," said Cooley, beckoning to the waitress.

"Billy here is a local historian and has a great interest in Georgian Dublin," explained Martin when they had ordered.

"Did Martin tell you what we were looking for?" asked Doyler.

"Yes," said Billy. "He told me your boss is researching ghosts, ghouls and goblins and the like."

"Yes, sort of," said Cooley. "Concentrating more on vampires."

Billy pulled out a tattered notebook.

"There are very few tales as such about vampires. Now ghosts, headless horsemen, phantom horses, banshees – there are plenty of stories about them . . ."

Doyler sighed, feeling this meeting might turn out to be a total waste of time.

Billy put on his glasses. One of the lenses was cracked and a pin was holding the right arm of the glasses where a screw should have been. "Sometimes I find it hard to read my own writing," he said.

"I'm not surprised," Doyler muttered under this breath.

Billy put down his notes as the waitress arrived with their order.

"There's nothing like a cheese sandwich with a spread of English mustard. Sometimes I add a bit of onion if I'm making it for myself at home. My wife, may the Lord rest her soul, was a great cook. She could make a meal out of anything. In those days there wasn't much but somehow she always managed to put a good dinner on the table for the two of us. She had a kind heart, a gentle soul. She would feed the sparrows with the crumbs. Now I'm talking of a time before it was fashionable to do it."

Doyler prodded Cooley.

"You were about to tell us a vampire story," sad Cooley.

"Oh yes," said the old man, perusing his notes.

"You're not getting a free lunch for nothing," Martin teased.

"Yes, well back to my notes. These notes were written in 1963 shortly after poor President Kennedy was assassinated. I remember exactly what I was doing on that day. That's not bad for a man who will be eighty next birthday."

"Billy, you're a topper. Now will you tell these two spook-hunters the vampire story!" said Martin.

Doyler blew his nose hard out of frustration.

"These notes were taken from the files of the Royal Dublin Constabulary. They were stored in Dublin Castle." He looked at the men. "Well, in 1897 four young men were arrested in Church Street. There were two bodies found on the night. One was an English professor who spent a great deal of time abroad in Europe. He lay on the ground stabbed to death by a cane-sword. These are my notes, mind you. I like to write things down my way if you get my meaning."

"We do," said Cooley.

"Well, the other victim was a young woman. The strange thing was she died of a bite to the neck. According to the police report she seemed to have lost a great deal of blood."

Doyler and Cooley glanced at each other.

"Fascinating, don't you think?" said Billy.

"Yes, please go on," said Doyler.

"Well, the young men were arrested. At their trial they told the court that the professor was a vampire hunter and that they were chasing down a Baron Rellick, who they claimed was a vampire that had killed several people in London before coming to Dublin. They had discovered the vampire was using the crypt in St Michan's as his resting place."

"St Michan's!" exclaimed Doyler. "Of course, a perfect place for a vampire to hide."

"What happened the young men?" asked Martin.

"I have no idea," said Billy. "The files had several pages torn out. I checked other volumes but could find nothing about that case. Did you know that the Duke of Wellington was born in Dublin?"

"Yes, we did," said Doyler.

"There's a fascinating story about the monument in the Phoenix Park . . ."

"Well, we'd love to hear about it sometime," said Doyler, "but we have to go now. We have to attend to some very important business."

"Well, it was lovely to sit here and chat with you fine gents."

"The pleasure was ours," Cooley shook his hand. "We'd better go. Martin, will you see that Mister Roche gets home?" Martin nodded. Cooley took out twenty pounds. "Here you are."

"What's that for?" asked Billy.

"For the information. The stories," said Doyler.

"I'm not taking that," said Billy. "Sure if I got a penny for every story I told I'd be a millionaire!"

"Take it," Cooley insisted. "Buy yourself a book."

"Well, I'm in the right place," smiled Billy.

"Sorry we have to rush," said Doyler. They said their goodbyes and left.

When they got out on the quays they patted each other on the back. "That was a stroke of luck," said Cooley. "See, I told you Martin was good at ferreting out the right people."

"It was a bit like pulling teeth getting the right information out of him," Doyler grinned.

"While it's still light, let's get over to St Michan's. It's only a short walk," said Cooley.

They hurried up along the quays past the Four Courts, left Inns Quay and turned up Church Street. They could see St Michan's on the left, the Bridewell police station on the right. St Michan's seemed almost dwarfed by the new buildings that had mushroomed nearby. The gate was open. They entered the church.

"Leave it to me," said Doyler. There were two friendly gentlemen sitting behind a desk in a small shop. A few souvenirs, books and postcards were for sale there. "Gentlemen," said Doyler interrupting the men who were making themselves a cup of tea. He smiled broadly, "You can't beat a cup of tea." The men smiled back.

"I'm afraid the guided tours are finished for the day. But if you would care to look around the church you can do so for free."

"That's very kind of you," said Doyler, "but we'd like to contribute to the upkeep of the place." He took out two pound coins and placed them on the counter. "My friend and I are doing some research – we're writers, you know!" Cooley looked at him. "Yeah, we write history books."

"How very interesting," said one of the elderly gents.

"I don't suppose you could squeeze a cup of tea out of the pot for my friend and me."

"Certainly," said the man, pouring tea for them and giving them biscuits.

"With all the building going on, the city gets very dusty at times," said Doyler as he dipped the chocolate biscuit into his mug of tea.

"Well, we can tell you a little about St Michan's church and its history if you like."

"Oh great, that's why we're here," said Doyler. "Before you begin perhaps my friend could have a quick peek at the vaults – he's been dying to see the mummies for years and we have to go abroad tomorrow – otherwise we'd come back when the guide was here."

"Well, I suppose that would be okay since you're doing research and all," said one of the men.

"Off you go," said Doyler to Cooley. "I'll take some notes

here." He pulled out a stump of a pencil and an envelope he had in his jacket pocket. He sucked the top of the pencil and smiled at Cooley. "I'm all set."

"Thanks very much," said Cooley, showing his annoyance.

"You will have to go outside the church. On the side you will see the iron doors, pull the bolt across and there are steps that lead down to the vaults. Do mind your head on the way down!"

"And your neck," grinned Doyler.

"His neck?" asked one of the men.

"Oh nothing, it's just a joke between us. Now, tell me all about this fine church," said Doyler as he sat on a chair and drank his tea.

"The church itself was built in 1095. For centuries it was the only church on the north side of the Liffey. I must show you the beautiful organ. It was refurbished in 1952. It's here since 1724. It is said that Frederick Handel played it while in Dublin, while preparing for his production of the Messiah. The marvellous wooden carving of seventeen musical instruments is all carved out of a single piece of wood."

"Fascinating," said Doyler as he poured himself more tea.

"The carving was made in 1724 . . ."

Doyler sat and listened, pretending to take notes, wishing Cooley would hurry up. Then the door opened quickly. A very pale-looking Cooley stood there wide-eyed. Doyler looked at him. Cooley patted the left side of his chest, indicating he had something in his inside pocket. Doyler looked at his watch.

"Would you look at the time. We really must go – time flies when you're having fun." They thanked the men and hurried out of the church. "Did you get it?" Doyler asked. Cooley saw a cab.

"Taxi!" he yelled, waving his arms frantically. They sat in the back of the cab. Cooley said nothing.

"You look like you've seen a ghost," said Doyler.

Cooley was trembling all over. "I need a drink, but I want to get as far away from those crypts as possible." They asked the taxi driver to bring them to St. Stephen's Green. From there they walked down a favourite pub of theirs.

After Cooley had drunk down a pint of Guinness in two gulps he began to feel a bit more at ease – although his hands were still trembling. "You're a right so-and-so asking me to go alone down there," he snapped.

"Look Cooley, you're younger, slimmer and fitter, and you know I have a bad ankle. Besides I had to keep those two old boyos occupied in case they got suspicious." Cooley picked up his second pint. "Think of the money," said Doyler.

"It was freaky, I tell you, descending those old steps and

going along that long corridor with burial chambers on either side. Those mummified bodies were in a chamber at the end of the corridor to the left. Directly opposite, in another chamber were coffins heaped on top of one another. It was there I spied a black coffin that was carefully concealed behind the other coffins. I tell you the sweat was pouring down my face. My heart was pounding, I thought my chest would burst with all the pounding. When I lifted up the lid of the black coffin, there he lay like a black leech, with blood on his lips. His fangs were protruding over his lower lip. I was scared witless in case he woke up. He looked as still as stone. I reached carefully inside the nearest pocket. There was a handkerchief in it. Then I felt inside his coat and found the piece of paper in the pocket. I tell you, I didn't hang around. I was out of there like a shot. I thanked the good Lord to have got up those steps and back out into the fresh air in one piece."

"Let's see it."

Cooley carefully removed the ancient paper. Doyler nervously opened it out. The script was beautifully done. It was written in Latin.

"Cooley, my boy, we've hit the jackpot."

"Quick, put it away," said Cooley anxiously.

Inspector Wilson and Detective McGuire had come in and were making for their table.

"Afternoon, Doyle! Collins!"

"Hello, Inspector. Didn't know you people drank on duty!" Doyler quipped.

"What were you two fellows doing over at St. Michan's today?" said McGuire. "We tailed you so don't deny it."

"We were just acting like tourists," said Cooley. "We've wanted to visit the place for ages."

"Yes," said Doyler. "To shake hands with the mummy!"

"What kind of research were you doing there, you pair of writers? Yes, I spoke to the attendants after you two left," said Inspector Wilson sternly.

"Listen, Inspector. It's a free country. Surely a man can visit historical sites without being spied on by the law!" Doyler protested.

"What were you trying to hide when we arrived?" asked McGuire.

"Nothing," said Cooley.

The two policemen sat down. "Listen, lads. We're investigating several incidents and bizarre killings in the city. If you lads are holding anything back from us –"

Doyler's mobile phone rang. "Excuse me, Inspector. Hello? Oh, Doctor Drachler. Yes, we have very good news for you! I'll call over later. Bye."

"What's the very good news you have for the Doctor?" asked McGuire.

"It's personal," said Doyler.

"Listen," said McGuire, holding back his anger with difficulty. "We can do this two ways, the easy way or the hard way. Perhaps you'd prefer to come down to the station with us now!"

"On what charge?" asked Doyler defiantly.

"In connection with a recent spate of killings."

"Show it to them," said Cooley.

They pulled out the faded document. The Inspector carefully opened it. They explained it was some kind of ancient prescription, a homeopathic formula that Madame Kinski needed for some rare blood disease. Wilson looked at McGuire. It certainly looked old and they could see it was written in Latin, probably a quill pen was used.

"Did you find this in St. Michan's?" the Inspector probed.

"Sort of," said Doyler.

"Another life could be in danger tonight," snapped McGuire. "Now, where did you get it?"

"Inspector, I'm sure the killer you are after is the same one I took this from. According to Doctor Drachler his name is Baron Rellick and he's a . . ."

"Go on," said McGuire.

"A vampire!" said Cooley nervously. "Honestly, I've seen him – it!"

"You mean he's still there!" said Wilson.

"Yes, and I'll swear to it on my dear mother's grave," said Cooley. "He's lying in a black coffin in a dead sleep."

The Inspector took a deep breath and looked at McGuire. "Should we call for back-up?"

"I think we should check it out first."

The Inspector put the parchment into his inside pocket.

"Hey, that's ours, We need it." Doyler protested.

"You will get it after you show us where this Baron Rellick is hiding."

"He's down in those vaults, honest!" Cooley trembled at the thought of it.

"Show us," said McGuire.

"I'm not going back there, neither for love nor money."

"If you two don't want to spend the night in prison, you'll do as you're told."

"Police brutality," Doyler mumbled.

"Let's go," said the Inspector.

They took the police car up to St. Michan's. Doyler and Cooley sat quietly in the back, feeling very nervous. The closer they got to St. Michan's the worse Cooley felt. "Look," said Cooley panicking, "the sun has set." The car pulled up outside the old church. There were chains on the front gate.

"Get out of the car," said McGuire.

"It's all locked up," said Doyler. "We can call back tomorrow morning." Cooley was still in the back of the car.

"Out!" said the Inspector. Cooley reluctantly left the safety of the car. "Remember you are helping with police work. There might even be a reward for you," said the Inspector.

"Thanks, but I'd rather be at the pictures right now,"

Cooley muttered. "One minute they're threatening us with gaol; the next they're offering us a reward."

McGuire scaled the iron railings and jumped to the ground. "You two next."

"Please, Inspector, at my age – to be climbing those dangerous railings – it's just not on," said Doyler. McGuire called to them, pointing to an easier place to climb into the church grounds. They had no choice but to do what the police had demanded. McGuire looked at Cooley.

"There," Cooley pointed at the iron gates that protruded from the ground, "that's the way down to the vaults." McGuire picked up a medium-sized granite rock and proceeded to hit the lock on the bolted doors.

"Breaking and entering," Doyler sneered. The lock finally snapped open.

"You missed your vocation," said Cooley. "You could have been a burglar."

"Very funny," said McGuire as he lifted up the two iron doors.

A musty odour assailed their nostrils. The detective shone his torch down the steps and pulled out a gun. "Follow me," said McGuire.

Doyler pleaded with the Inspector but his words fell on deaf ears.

"Move!" snapped Wilson.

"Why do I have to go down?" whined Doyler. "I've never been down there before."

"Well, here's your chance," said the Inspector. "Now hurry up."

Once down the steps they moved forward slowly along the passageway. The small torch the Inspector had was the only source of light in the inky-black crypt. They were all uneasy as the beam of light spotlighted the chamber where the ebony coffin was.

"Can we go now?" asked Doyler. "You've found it." McGuire groped about over the old crumbling coffins towards the black one. His hands trembled. With one hand on the lid and the other with his gun ready to fire he pulled up the coffin lid.

"Aaahh," he yelled, as hundreds of rat scrambled out of the coffin. He let off a shot. Doyler reached into his pocket, felt the cross he had placed there earlier, pulled it out and held it with both hands in front of him. The Inspector and Cooley cowered.

"It's empty. Let's get the hell out of here," McGuire shouted. They ran along the passageway and up the stairs, Doyler banging his head on the way out and cutting his forehead.

"Ouch," he moaned.

"Sorry, Inspector," said McGuire, struggling for breath. "I didn't mean to shoot off my pistol, but when I saw all those rats . . ."

"Don't worry. It put the wind up me too." They looked at Cooley.

"There was no vampire lying in the coffin," said McGuire.

"Well?" asked the Inspector.

"Don't you see, Inspector. It's up and about! I swear I saw it earlier. Believe me!"

"Let's pay a visit to Madame Kinski and the Doctor. Somebody better have some satisfactory answers for me before this night is out. I don't want any more killings in our city by no freaking vampire," said the Inspector. They tried to cover up their tracks as best they could then headed for the Shelbourne Hotel, where Madame Kinski was staying.

"We're here to see Doctor Drachler," said McGuire to the hotel receptionist. The receptionist phoned up to their room.

"Sorry, sir. There's no answer."

"Try again! Tell Madame Kinski or Doctor Drachler that Inspector Wilson needs to speak to them urgently!"

"Never mind, we'll go on up," insisted the Inspector.

The receptionist looked blankly at the porter beside her who had an equally blank expression on his face.

"What's going on? We need to speak to the Doctor urgently," Inspector Wilson snapped.

"But, sir . . ." the girl stammered, "an Inspector Wilson has already called."

"What?!" he exclaimed.

"He asked for somewhere private to have an urgent meeting with the Doctor," she added.

"Is he still here?" demanded McGuire.

"Come to think of it, he didn't look very much like a policeman," the porter remarked, "but it's hard to tell nowadays."

"Show me the room! Immediately!" ordered the Inspector.

"He said under no circumstances were they to be disturbed."

"I am Inspector Wilson. Hurry, a man's life may be at stake," he yelled. The porter grabbed a bunch of keys.

"Follow me. They're in a small conference room up the stairs on the left."

They hurried up the stairs. The porter was about to knock on the door, but McGuire stopped him. "Open it," he whispered. The porter rumbled a bit, then placed the correct key in the door and turned it in the lock. McGuire pushed in the door. He and Wilson rushed into the room. They could see a man lying on the floor and another bent over him.

It was the vampire. He raised his head and glowered at them. His anger intensified, he hissed, blood running from his mouth. Then he smiled an evil grin. "I have sucked the vital fluid out of Doctor Drachler."

"You fiend," shouted Wilson as the vampire threw a chair at him. McGuire let off a shot which hit the vampire in the shoulder.

"You think bullets can kill me," he growled, then jumped onto the Inspector and gripped him by the throat. Doyler pulled out the crucifix and pushed it into the vampire's face. The vampire jerked back. There was a scar where the cross had touched him. His face hardened with anger. "I will get you all for this." He threw another chair at the window, leapt through, then hurried up the wall and onto the roof. McGuire took another shot at him but he was nowhere to be seen. They checked the doctor who was lying unconscious. McGuire called for an ambulance, then they hurried up to Madame Kinski's room. They pounded on her door. There was no answer. Quickly they ordered the porter to open the door. They rushed inside. They couldn't believe their eyes.

Madame Kinski sat by the window with pen and paper in her hands.

"Gentlemen!"

They could see she was chained by her leg to the bed-post. A cross was taped beside the lock on the chain.

"What's going on here?" asked the Inspector.

"I shall explain later. Where is Alex? The Doctor? He went down to meet you – he said you have what I'm looking for."

"We have," said the Inspector, "but I've some bad news for you. The Doctor was attacked by Baron Rellick, masquerading as me. God only knows how he knew my name." He sighed deeply.

"No!" sobbed Frederika. "Is he . . .?"

"No, he's alive. The ambulance is on its way."

"You must get him a blood transfusion immediately," she shouted. "Untie me at once! Alex has the key."

McGuire returned to where Doctor Drachler was lying, felt around in his pockets and found the key for the lock. He hurried back to the room and undid the chain and lock around Madame Kinski's ankle.

"It may not be too late," she said to herself.

"Madame Kinski, we will have to ask you to accompany us down to the station."

"No, Inspector, I cannot join you. I must do something I should have done a long time ago," she hissed. They could see two fangs appear. She turned to the window and jumped through it.

"My God," yelled Doyler. "She's a vampire too."

She leaped to the ground, startling a passer-by who ran shrieking down the road. Frederika scanned the darkness with amber eyes. She could sense the Baron was nearby. Then she pinpointed him on a distant roof. He was smiling as if he was half expecting her. She quickly climbed a drainpipe and was soon up on the roof of the hotel. There was the sound of an ambulance and a police car.

"I will give him two days before your darling Doctor becomes like us," the Baron shouted at her. Frederika shrieked and ran to the edge of the building, then leaped across to the far building. Two people looking in the window of James Adam's auction rooms suddenly heard a crash and a slate from the roof fell beside them. The Baron ran across the roofs, Frederika in hot pursuit. They leaped effortlessly from roof to roof. A security man on duty on one of the buildings, watching while two men repaired a roof that was damaged by a fire days earlier, noticed a man running towards them.

"What the heck?" said the security man. "Where do you think you're going?" He stepped in front of the Baron. The Baron knocked him off the roof. The security man screamed as he hurtled towards certain death. The next minute he felt someone grip him. Frederika had dived down and caught him just in time.

"My God, are you my guardian angel?" said the poor man to her.

"Perhaps," she smiled. She eased him to the street, then climbed back up the building. As she reached the top a foot stepped hard first on one hand, then on the other.

"Dear Frederika, you and I could have made a wonderful couple. What a pity it should end like this."

"Never! You are a vicious killer, a black-hearted fiend!" she cried.

"Brave words for one about to fall to her death. Those old iron railings below look very sharp from here. It won't be a pretty sight to see you impaled on them." He stamped hard on her hands.

Frederika began to lose her grip.

"Stop," yelled a voice from behind. It was the security man with Inspector Wilson, Detective McGuire and the other two workers. McGuire had borrowed Doyler's cross and was holding it in his hand and walking towards the Baron. Frederika took advantage of the diversion, knocked the Baron off balance and freed her hand. The Baron staggered on the edge and tried to find his balance. McGuire threw the crucifix at him. A devilish scream came from the Baron, as he fell from the roof and impaled himself on the railings below. The death he had planned for Frederika had become his fate.

The Inspector and the security man helped Frederika back up onto the roof.

"Are you my guardian angel?" she asked the security man. He grinned.

"One good turn deserves another."

"Are you all right?" the Inspector asked. She looked at her bruised hands.

"I'll live," she smiled.

The Inspector looked down at the body of Baron Rellick which was disintegrating in front of their very eyes. Moments later there was nothing to show that he was ever there, except for some torn clothing. The Inspector breathed a sigh of relief knowing that Baron Rellick's reign of terror had ended.

"Can you please take me to the hospital where they are keeping dear Alex?" Frederika asked.

"I'll find out which hospital he's been taken to," said McGuire.

# Chapter 11

Two weeks later, the Shelbourne Hotel

Frederika, Doctor Drachler, Doyler and Cooley were joined for breakfast by Inspector Wilson and Detective McGuire. "That was a splendid breakfast," said Doyler, "but I wouldn't mind another pot of tea. Tea is great to lubricate the tongue," he added.

"What time is your flight?" asked Inspector Wilson.

"Not until one-thirty," said the Doctor. "We stay two days in London. Frederika is being interviewed by the Arts Show for BBC2."

"Do you want me to say I'm a vampire?" she teased the doctor. He smiled.

"Let's just stick to talking about your writing."

"Well, you've made a remarkable recovery," said McGuire to the Doctor.

"When the source of the evil is destroyed, its immediate victims are set free," replied the Doctor.

"Does that include you, Madame?" asked the Inspector.

"It does, indeed. I will live out a normal life in this twenty-first century, hopefully with my dear Alex."

The others smiled and looked at each other.

"Before I forget . . ." said the Doctor. He wrote two cheques, one for Doyler and one for Cooley. Their eyes widened when they saw they were for two thousand pounds each.

"Thanks very much," beamed Doyler. "Most generous."

"Oh, by the way, you two," said McGuire, looking at them, "call to the station later on. There's a reward for you for helping us solve a major crime."

Doyler and Cooley smiled and gave each other the thumbs up.

"Well, we must be away," said the Inspector. "Thanks for all your help. Oh I nearly forgot!" He handed them the parchment.

"Thank you, Inspector," said Frederika. "Thankfully I will not need it any more. But I will make sure it gets a good home in the library of ancient manuscripts in Rome." They said their farewells.

"Thank you, Doyler and Cooley. You have always come up trumps for me," said the Doctor shaking their hands warmly.

Frederika kissed them tenderly. "Goodbye and thank you," she smiled.

"Well, let's hope you have enough material for a new

book out of all the experiences you've had," Cooley quipped.

"Indeed," she smiled, "I may even call it The Irish Vampire Hunters."

"Just leave us out of it," said Doyler. "I've had enough dealings with vampires to last me a lifetime. No offence meant!"

The End